I0645229

It couldn't be legit, it was just too weird…

This was too weird. What were the odds of there being a witness at this place at the same time as them? Maggie knew them to be astronomical. It had to be some kind of gag. She stood. "We need to go."

"Wait a sec, Mags. This is legit. I know you won't believe it, but I spoke to a woman on the phone earlier and arranged to meet her here. It was the plan to get you in a better mood as well as meet with a potential witness." He glanced up at the girl and back at Maggie. "This must be her."

"Yes, that was me," the girl said. "I called in because I heard a guy talking on the phone about a gun and then he hung up and darted to the parking lot. He got into a black Plymouth Charger. I wrote down the tag number to call it in. I was afraid he might be some kind of criminal out to hurt someone."

"Why didn't you just call in to a dispatcher and give the number?" Maggie asked.

"I was scared. He saw me as I was waiting to use the phone because the battery was dead on mine. I figured I'd meet with an officer and give it over that way. You know, in exchange for some kind of protection if the guy comes after me."

Maggie thought it all sounded unbelievable and unreliable, but then she remembered her gut feeling about the man on the phone being on the up and up so she stayed seated and continued to eat her ice cream. "What's the tag info?"

The girl gave the number and Jacob called it in.

After taking a formal statement from the girl, including her name and address, Jacob let her go with a promise that he'd arrange for extra drive-bys on her street by the police department for the next few nights.

Almost as soon as she was gone, the dispatcher rang back with the information on the driver.

Jacob tossed his cup and spoon in the trash. "Ready to roll? We have a couple of uniforms meeting us at the address on the car's registration."

"Then let's go." Maggie threw away her container as well and followed Jacob to his car.

She wondered exactly who and what they would find there—and if she was about to come face to face with at least one of the people who played a part in the death of Drusilla.

No one liked Drusilla Isaacs. She spent a lifetime alienating people, as if making the most enemies was a personal goal. Now she's dead. Shot, stabbed, and her neck broken…and that's what the coroner can tell from a first look. It's up to Maggie Blaine—former friend and one-time victim of the odious Drusilla—and Maggie's partner, Jacob Brown, to figure out who, out of a seemingly endless list of suspects, would carry out such heinous acts. Their choices are varied. From Drusilla's husbands—the former and the current—to the women in her life—her secretary, the mother of her husband's son, or the new wife of her ex-husband. There's also another option. A serial killer who randomly appears to insert himself into the mix. A tale of murder, gems, drugs, illicit sex, and a cast of villains who all have one thing in common—their hatred of Drusilla Isaacs.

Overkill is intriguing, charming, fast paced, and full of surprises. This one that will catch and hold your interest from the very first page. ~ *Regan Murphy, The Review Team of Taylor Jones & Regan Murphy*

ACKNOWLEDGMENTS

I'd like to thank two readers and subscribers to my newsletter, Jeffery Stutsman and Joy Winslow, for allowing me to use their names for two of the characters in this tale. It was fun to include them, and I'm grateful to them.

I am also indebted to a number of my law enforcement friends for their "shop talk" that I used as inspiration for the way my detectives interact with each other as well as the suspects.

Other books by
Sherry Fowler Chancellor

Senior Assassin

The Eisenger Element

Till Murder Do Us Part

Cowboy Boots on the Ground

OVERKILL

Sherry Fowler Chancellor

A Black Opal Books Publication

DEDICATION

*To my court security friends at the Winston E. Arnow
Federal Building in Pensacola, Florida.
You all light up my life.*

CHAPTER 1

The dead woman lay sprawled on the dry grass near the sidewalk with her neck canted to the side at an impossible angle. Blood surrounded her, puddled mostly around her head, but there was also some around her upper torso. One breast had escaped from her too-low-cut blouse, and her skirt barely covered whatever panties she might have on. A black stiletto sat a few feet away, a mate to the one on her foot. Festively painted lime green toenails on the bare one seemed to mock the horrific scene.

Detective Maggie Blaine knew the deceased well and had even once thought of her as a friend. After all the history between them, it was hard for Maggie to muster any sadness at the lady's demise. A pang of regret for what might have been passed over her. She stepped back, her head reeling.

Her partner, Jacob Brown, took her by the elbow. "You okay, Mags?"

"Fine. I'm fine." She adjusted the service weapon at her waist and held herself together.

"You're pale and shaky. This isn't your first rodeo so why the nerves?" he asked.

Maggie shook her head. "I know—sorry—I *knew* her."

"You knew this woman dressed in early 1970s hooker garb? How's that?"

"She's an accountant. Always did wear inappropriate clothes." Maggie tried not to smile at her partner's characterization of Drusilla's wardrobe. Many times she wanted to have a discussion with her former friend about professionalism.

"Should I call the captain and have her send someone else to partner me on this?"

"No, no. I'll be all right. It's just a bit of a shock, is all."

Jacob looked her in the eye as if assessing her condition. "You don't think you have a conflict in investigating?"

"Back off, Brown. I said I'm fine." Maggie knelt down beside the body and whispered, "You probably had it coming. I'm sorry it happened anyway. I wish you'd learned sooner."

"Excuse me, Detective." Miguel Martinez, the medical examiner, crouched beside her. "Want to give me a chance once you're done with the last rites?"

"Very funny, Doc." Maggie stood and smoothed her slacks. "What do you think is the cause of death?"

"I'll know more when I can get a better look at her at the morgue. Looks like some stab wounds and a broken neck but I'll need to do a full workup before I know what actually killed her."

"Anyone else on the slab or can we come by later?" Jacob asked.

"She's the only customer today so far." Martinez rose. "But I imagine the crime scene guys will take a while, so give me a couple of hours to get her in and start the work." He turned and moved over to talk to the photographer.

Maggie shrugged. "Let's do some canvassing and see if anyone saw anything."

"Already have some patrolmen working that apartment complex over there." Jacob pointed across the road to a set of pale blue clapboard buildings.

"Then let's hit the other side." Maggie took a step onto the sidewalk.

A man with tightly-curled gray hair who reeked of stale beer and vomit staggered toward her. "Hey, lady, is that Drusilla Isaacs?"

His words were slurred, but she understood them easily enough.

"I can't confirm or deny until the next of kin is notified."

The man spat on the ground. "No need. I'd know that bitch anywhere. Can't say I'll be sad to see her go." He wheezed out a laugh that ended in a coughing fit. When he recovered, he said, "I can bet that next of kin of hers won't care either. Other than his meal ticket being gone."

"You know her next of kin?"

"So it *is* her?" He laughed again.

"What do you know? Did you see anything?" Jacob walked over to where the man stood on the side of the road.

"Didn't see nothing here, but I can tell ye, that ole man of hers will be glad to have her gone. The old sod never wanted to marry her anyway, but she done tol' him he'd have to move on out o' her house if'n he didn't ask her to be his bride. Next thing ye knew, that broad had a ring on her finger." He leaned toward Maggie and exhaled a breath that could have knocked a bull moose on its keister. "Ye don' look the type to be wanting to marry a man who didn't want ye. What kind of woman would do that?"

"I'm sure I don't know, sir, but I wasn't aware she was married." Maggie realized her mistake as soon as the words left her mouth. She'd just admitted she knew the victim and to a potential witness at that.

"Oh, yeah. Married they was. Miserable, but married." The old guy snickered again then was caught up in another coughing fit. When he could speak again, he waved his hands in the air as if trying to maintain control. "But I reckon they's all like that. Marriages, I mean."

Maggie shook her head and glanced at her partner. "I'm going to let you interview the philosopher while I canvass."

"Thanks. I owe you for that." Jacob took out his notepad and pencil.

Leaving him to it, Maggie opened the screen and knocked on the door of the small Craftsman house closest to the place where Drusilla died.

A voice called out, "Wait one moment, I'm on the way."

At the moment Maggie decided she should knock again, the wooden door opened. An elderly African American woman stood inside. She wore a bathrobe and a pair of fluffy slippers that had seen much better days. What fluff was left was bedraggled and sad. "May I help you, young lady?"

Pulling back her jacket, Maggie showed the badge at her waist to the woman and tilted her head toward the murder scene. "I'm Detective Blaine and wondered if you saw anything happening across the street. We're checking with all the neighbors."

The woman opened the creaky screen door. "You want to come in for some iced tea? It's mighty hot out there."

"No, thank you. Unless you saw something you need

to tell me about. I can then sit with you to discuss it."

The lady seemed disappointed. Perhaps she didn't get many visitors. Maggie's heart hurt for her if she was lonely. She knew how that could be.

"I didn't see anything." The woman took off her glasses. "Look at these. So thick they hurt my nose. I don't wear them like I should. Maybe if I'd had them on, I might've seen something."

"That's all right." Maggie turned to go.

"But I *did* maybe hear something."

Maggie looked back. "Really?"

"Come on in, and I'll tell you all about it." The lady stepped back to let Maggie in. "I'm Hattie Simpkins."

Not sure if Mrs. Simpkins was telling her the truth or merely wanted someone to chat with, Maggie had to take the chance the lady knew something. She followed her hostess inside.

The interior of the home was dark and dingy. Maggie supposed it was because the woman couldn't see very well and the paneling in her living room was a deep brown.

Maybe she didn't realize how much it needed a cleaning or even a lamp or two turned on.

Moving a small gray tabby cat aside in order to take the chair indicated by Mrs. Simpkins, Maggie sat. The cat wound itself around her ankles.

"I'll get the tea. Don't let Mordecai bother you too much."

While Mrs. Simpkins was in the kitchen, Maggie picked up the kitty and petted it. "You're a sweet thing, aren't you?"

When the elderly lady shuffled back in with two glasses of tea, she smiled at the cat on Maggie's lap. "That boy there is a troublemaker."

"Seems to me he's a sweetie." Maggie set him on the floor and focused on her notepad as Mrs. Simpkins put one of the glasses on the table beside Maggie.

The older lady looked at the animal with sheer love reflected in her eyes. "Don't be lettin' that creature trick you."

Glad she had at least an animal companion, Maggie said, "What did you hear outside today, Mrs. Simpkins?"

"I was out on my porch a couple of times. That Drusilla's office is right down the road, and she prances by here once in a while. She walked past today two times. I heard her out there arguing with someone early this morning."

"Did you know the person she was speaking with?"

"No. It was a man, but I have no idea who. She has that shrill voice, so I knew it was her."

"Could you describe the man?" Maggie knew the lady was practically blind, but she had to ask the question.

"Only to say he was tall and 'big-boned' as my mother would have said."

"No hair color?"

"Couldn't tell." Mrs. Simpkins took a sip of her tea.

"But it wasn't her husband. This was a white man."

"Okay. Good. That's good." Maggie made some notes. "What about the other time you said Drusilla came by your house today. What did you hear then?"

"Just her talking on that phone she's always on. I never saw anyone love a phone like that lady do. She paces on the sidewalk sometimes talking on that thing. Don't know why she doesn't stay in that office of hers, instead of being out here disturbing the peace."

Maggie held back a laugh, as she had to agree with the woman. Back when she and Drusilla were what she thought were friends, they would sometimes go to lunch together. Drusilla was always more concerned about watching her phone for texts and calls than chatting with the person sitting at the same table with her.

"Was there anything about the conversation that you heard that you think I should know?" Maggie asked.

"I couldn't hear it all. Something about money being owed to her, and she was going to get a lawyer and some other stuff like that. Real threatening, like."

"Did she mention any names?"

"No, honey, she didn't. That was all I heard. Don't know who she was talking to." Mrs. Simpkins took another swallow of her tea and rattled the ice. She nodded at Maggie's still half-full glass. "You want some more?"

"No. Thank you." Maggie flipped her notebook closed. "This helps. If you think of anything else that you heard, call me, please." She handed Mrs. Simpkins one of her cards. "I answer this number anytime it rings."

"Must you go so soon?"

Maggie stood. "Yes. I appreciate the tea, but I need to keep talking to people. We've got to find out who killed her, so I must go."

"I hope you'll come back sometime when you have a little time to visit." Mrs. Simpkins walked Maggie to the door with Mordecai following his owner as she shuffled along.

"I'd love to. My next day off, I'll come by, and you can tell me about all the people I noticed in the photos you have on the wall."

"That would be mighty kind of you. I have to say, it sometimes gets lonely now that my children are all grown and living with their own families." She reached down and picked up the cat. "I'm lucky to have Mordecai here."

Maggie patted the cat's head. "I'm glad he's good company. I'll be seeing you soon."

"I wish you luck on your task finding that Drusilla's killer. She made new enemies every day, so you have a hard case to work." Mrs. Simpkins turned and carried her cat back inside.

Quite sure the old woman was right, Maggie turned to look for her partner.

∽∾∽

Back at the station, Maggie and Jacob set out all their notes, as well as the canvassing officers' notes, and began to draw a time line of what they'd discovered. The white dry-erase board was soon covered with red, green, and blue markings as they sorted through the information.

In the midst of their work, the phone on Maggie's desk rang.

"Detective Blaine? It's Doc Martinez. Got you a cause of death. It's a doozy."

"Really? What?"

"Come on down to the morgue. This you need to see." The doctor hung up. He had to know that was the fastest way to get her down there. The man was incorrigible.

"Let's get to the morgue. Doc's playing games again." Maggie grabbed her keys and poked Jacob on the arm. "Don't dally."

"I never dally." He followed her out to the parking lot. "What's the big rush?"

"He said our cause of death is a doozy. I want to see exactly what that medical term means."

They drove the few miles to the hospital where the morgue was located and made their way to the bottom floor of the facility.

Inside the morgue, Martinez led them to the table where Drusilla lay.

Maggie had to cover her mouth. It was always hard to visit this place but when it was someone she knew on the slab it made it that much harder. True, she and Drusilla had fallen out long ago, but it was still mighty difficult to see her there with the Y-incision and the top of her skull still in the pan on the side table.

"What's the cause of death?" she asked.

"You're looking pale again, Blaine. You sure you want to be on this case?" Jacob asked.

"I'm fine."

"Your face is the same color as your hair. White on white isn't your color, darling." Jacob laughed. He leaned over the table and whispered to the coroner, "She likes to say she's a natural blonde, but have you ever seen hair *that* blonde?"

"Forget my hair. What's the cause of death?" Maggie asked.

"It's complicated, but I think I've narrowed it down." Martinez handed Maggie a piece of paper in a plastic bag. "Found this embedded in the fabric of her blouse in the back."

She peered at the paper. It had a number of brown smudges and streaks on it that she presumed was dried blood. After she read it, she passed it to Jacob. What it said was appropriate. Maggie knew from firsthand experience.

He read it out loud. "'Back stabber.'" Looking up at Martinez, he asked. "You found this actually *on* her back?"

"When the CSIs finished with the crime scene photos

and rolled her over, the note was stuck to the blood on her back. Her blouse was in shreds where someone had stabbed her six times."

"Was that the cause of death then?" Maggie asked.

"The stabbings would have eventually led to death. One of the wounds nicked her left kidney and another one hit the bottom of her heart. She was able to keep on her feet and walk out of her office."

"Wait. This happened at her office?" Jacobs asked.

"Yes. There was blood there. The scene was inspected once we realized the attack began there. It's kind of odd that there wasn't a bigger blood trail. One we could see. I guess most of it was soaked into the grass."

"We'll need to get over there, Maggie." Jacob touched Drusilla's toe. "Once we're done here, of course."

"It was obvious at the street scene that her neck was broken. Was that the cause of death?" Maggie asked.

"Well, it hastened it along, for sure."

"Will you get to it already? You're never this slow at telling us a cause." Maggie couldn't believe how Martinez was dragging this out.

"Have you ever read that book by Agatha Christie where everyone wants the victim dead, and they all had a hand in it?" Martinez asked.

"You mean *Murder on the Orient Express*?" Jacob asked.

Maggie's left eye started twitching. "Who cares

about some old novel? What. Is. The. Cause. Of. Death?"

"I'm trying to tell you. There may be plenty of suspects."

Maggie was incredulous. "So, you mean she died of more than one thing?"

"Ultimately, one thing killed her, but there were a number of things that *would* have before the day was over. She was stabbed, shot, poisoned, *and* her neck was broken. If I had to rank them, I say the broken neck did it." Martinez patted the steel table. "It's a tie on whether the gut shot or the poison would've been next. The longest one she could've survived was the stabbings. That would have been a slow bleed out."

"Well, you were right about one thing," Maggie said.

"What's that?" Jacob asked.

Maggie let out a bark of laughter. "He said the COD was a doozy."

"I suppose you'll want to know all about the poison. I've got the lab running some tests on it. There seems to have been more than one in her system."

"Can you give us a hint?" Jacob asked.

"Strychnine was the biggest component."

"Good God." Maggie paced the area beside the metal table. "Someone really hated her."

"Looks like at least four people," Jacob said. "We need to start talking to the husband as well as other family members."

"And her staff at the accounting office." Maggie followed Jacob to the door. She turned back to look at Martinez. "Email me that info on the poisons as soon as you get it."

"I will. I'll also let you know what evidence they get from the items they took from the stabbing scene."

"Thanks." Maggie walked back down the corridor with her brain spinning. How many enemies did Drusilla have? And why did they all pick the same day to try to do her in?

CHAPTER 2

Maggie and Jacob arrived at the house Drusilla shared with her husband. A dog barked incessantly as they stood on the porch. "Let's hope the animal has more bark than bite," Jacob said.

Maggie cringed at the sound. "And that it shuts up soon."

The door opened.

A man stood behind the storm door dressed in a pair of baggy workout shorts and nothing else. He had thick biceps and calves, but he'd somehow let his middle go to fat.

Maggie recognized him as a guy Drusilla used to date and must have married. His name was Curtis Beane.

He stared at Maggie for a moment as if trying to

place her. Without opening the door, he said, "Yeah, what you want?"

Jacob held up his badge. "Police. We need to talk about your wife."

Curtis opened the door. "Someone already came by to say she was dead. They said a cop made the identification. I told them which funeral home, so what else do you need?"

"We're the detectives investigating her death, and we have a few questions," Maggie said at the same moment a large wolfhound-type dog came galloping out past the master of the house.

Jacob stepped aside and pulled his weapon. "Call the dog off."

"That mutt won't hurt you. Don't be so jumpy," Curtis said.

"Then restrain him while we ask you our questions." Maggie wasn't afraid of the creature, but she didn't want to have to deal with it while speaking to the owner.

The man in question scratched his crotch. "Don't know what I can say to help you." He reached for the dog and grabbed it by the collar.

"Let us be the judge of that, please. It's standard procedure to talk to the family of the deceased. That would be you." Maggie couldn't believe the man didn't think they needed to speak to him. Was he truly an idiot? She'd met him once before. Way back when Drusilla and he started dating, but she hadn't been impressed. All he seemed to do was talk to her breasts. He never made eye contact and even bragged about cleaning Drusilla's shower in the nude as she watched. It was a weird conversation. Weirder than this one.

"Then I guess you can come in." He opened the door wider and allowed Maggie and Jacob to pass him into the hall.

Moving ahead of them and leading the way to the living room, Curtis said, "Sorry about the mess. I have my kid over, and Dru usually keeps the place clean. Don't know what I'll do now." He flopped into a blue recliner still holding on to the dog's collar.

"Can you go put the dog in another room?" Jacob asked.

Curtis let out a deep sigh before rising and taking the dog out.

While he was out, Maggie took a look around. The place was surprisingly shabbier than she would've imagined. The woman put on all the airs of someone who was successful and wealthy, but her home didn't match that persona. Perhaps she was more interested in spending money on other things.

Eventually, Curtis returned. As soon as he sat, he asked, "Am I a suspect?"

"Should you be?" Jacob asked.

"Hey, I watch TV. I know what you people think."

Great. Another person who thought television was the truth about criminal investigations. Of course, Curtis was right about one thing. The husband had to be ruled out immediately, as most murders were crimes of passion. And when love turned to hate, passions ran high.

"Do you know anyone who would want to harm your wife?" Maggie asked the question as she flipped open her notepad.

He leaned forward, resting his forearms on his thighs. "Lady, there were a lot of people who hated my wife. She had a way of making people dislike her."

"Do you have a list you could prepare for us?" Maggie asked.

"I know some of them but not all. Dru was all about Dru and what she needed or wanted. She didn't care who she stepped on to get it." Curtis ran his hand over his head. "I learned that early on."

"Yet you still married her," Jacob said.

"I did. Dru was relentless in getting what she wanted. At one time, I was what she wanted, and she didn't give up until I agreed to marry her."

"Why would you marry her if you knew she was like that?" Maggie continued to take notes on what he said.

"Didn't really want to marry her, but she talked me into letting my house be rented out on a year's lease. Once I was living here, she made the ultimatum. Marry her or move out."

Jacob let out a snort. "That's the lamest reason to get married that I've ever heard."

"Dru wanted a kid. I said we could have a kid without being married, but she wasn't having none of that. Heck, I already had one kid, it's not a big deal."

"But she wanted a marriage too?" Maggie asked.

"Yeah. I'm not big on the whole concept of it. My own parents weren't married, and me and my brother turned out okay."

Maggie wasn't too sure about that, but she let it go without comment. "Where were you today?"

"And so here it comes, huh? My alibi?" Curtis laughed. "My son is my alibi. I had him today. We were at the park for a while, and then went to have some ice cream."

"Anyone else with you? Or see you out at those places?" Jacob asked.

"In fact, yes. My son's mother met us at the ice cream place."

"You still see her socially?" Maggie made a note to visit the lady.

"She *is* the mother of my child." Curtis scratched his crotch again.

Trying to ignore his vulgar behavior, Maggie went on, "Did your wife get along with the child's mother?"

Curtis laughed and slapped his thigh. "What do you think? That they were the best of pals?"

"Of course not, but since you still see the woman, I was wondering how Drusilla felt about that." Maggie waited for an answer.

"She didn't know. It was easier not to tell her. I'd do

my thing with visiting my baby-mamma when Dru was at work. What she didn't know didn't hurt her."

"So you were in the habit of lying to your wife," Jacob asked.

"All men lie to their wives, bro." Curtis nodded at Jacob's hand. "I see you wear a wedding ring. Bet you lied to your wife within the last ten hours at least once."

Maggie glanced over at Jacob to see if he would react to that statement but to her amazement, he didn't even blink.

Instead, he said, "What I do isn't the issue."

Curtis turned to Maggie. "That means I'm right."

She changed the subject. "Please give us the names of the people who you think would wish your wife harm, and we also need the name and address of your son's mother. We'll need to talk to her as well."

He rose from the recliner again and lumbered over to the table to a pad of paper. Writing for a few moments, he eventually folded it in half and handed it to her. Before he sat again, Curtis asked, "Is there anything else you need from me? My boy's in there with the dog, and it's soon going to be time for me to feed him something." He glanced around for a moment as if lost, then added, "One thing Dru always took care of was food for the boy. Even if she was mad at me, she made sure little man was fed."

Maggie repressed a shudder at the term "little man" as that was one of her pet peeves. "Are you all right here with him? Did you need someone to assist you?"

"If you're asking me if I want Children and Family Services up in my business, that would be a no." He shuffled over to the hallway leading to the door. "I think we're done here. I got some hot dogs to cook."

Maggie and Jacob followed him out. Back on the porch, Jacob addressed the widower. "We'll probably have more questions. Please keep thinking of anyone who would want to harm your wife."

"If they still had local phone books, I'd tell you to start at 'A' and go to 'S' and probably every third name you came to would have had some issue with my wife at some point." He laughed as he closed the door in their faces.

Jacob shook his head. "Prime husband material there. Maybe you should set your cap for the obviously non-grieving spouse."

"Thanks for your concern about my love life, but that's one dude I've never cared for."

"So, you've had the privilege of meeting him before?" Jacob let Maggie lead the way to the curb and the car.

"Oh, yeah, when Drusilla first met him on an internet dating site. A few of us wanted to meet this paragon she was talking up, and so we went to dinner."

"How'd that work out?"

"None of us liked him. At all. First, he only spoke to our breasts and didn't look any of us in the eye. Then, when the bill came, the waitress placed it at his elbow.

He didn't even look at it but passed it to her as if he expected her to pay. No conversation about it or anything. Just poof, she was to pay. It made us all worry about what kind of man he was."

"What if they had some prearranged deal that they took turns paying and this was her turn?" Jacob opened the driver's side door.

"Even if they did, if she didn't want us to think he was a kept man, she should have said something about it being her turn. She knew exactly what we would all presume if she paid for the two of them."

Once Maggie was in the car and buckled in, Jacob said, "I'm a detective, and I can't even follow that female logic."

"It's easy to explain."

"It *is*?"

"Absolutely. It's the women's code. A real man could never understand it."

Jacob turned the key and started the car. "Then what chance do we mere mortals have?"

"None." She flipped her hair over her shoulder. "None at all."

He shook his head as he drove out of the neighborhood. "Where are we headed next? Who on the list our charming host gave us needs our attention?"

"I think we should pop by Drusilla's office and see it for ourselves. I'm not sure if the crime scene guys are done with it, but I'd like a look around."

"Did you ever visit the premises when the two of you were friends?"

"Nope. She moved offices since then. I got an invitation to her open house but didn't go. I figured I was still on her mailing list, even though I was certainly not going to attend, and she had to know it."

"Want to tell me exactly what happened between the two of you?"

Maggie darted a glance in his direction. "Not today but someday, I will."

"I'm going to hold you to that."

They continued on in silence until they reached the location of Drusilla's office. There was still a crime scene van parked in front of the building. "Good, they're still here. We won't have to get the landlord to let us in," Maggie said.

Inside the office, there were two CSIs busy collecting evidence. One man, one woman. She knew the woman but not the man.

"Just ignore us as we take a look around," Jacob said.

Maggie knelt beside a small puddle of what appeared to be dried blood. "Is this where she was stabbed?" she asked the woman, Angela.

"Yes, it looks like she was attacked as she walked past her desk. There's a handprint on the top where she must have staggered and caught herself."

The man glanced over and said, "There were a number of blood spots across the floor. We could trace her steps out the door, but then once she was on the grass, it was harder to spot it."

Maggie held her hand out. "I'm Detective Maggie Blaine, and this is my partner, Jacob Brown. Nice to meet you. When did you start with the department?"

"First week. Moved here from Lauderdale. I'm James Windsor."

"Hope you like it then. It's a bit different than south Florida." Maggie let go of his hand. "What else did you learn about what happened?"

"She seems to have made her way from the desk to outside wobbling here and there since she bumped against the wall in a couple of places as well. Just out-side, there was a lot of vomit. We bagged it and will test it against the samples Doc got in the autopsy." James walked over to the window. "She placed a hand here, too. No idea if she was looking out to see if her attacker was still out there."

"Any chance she used the phone?" Jacob asked.

"No sign of it." Angela shrugged. "I mean, no sign that she tried to call out after the attack. There are prints on the phone but nothing with blood or anything like that. More likely, she was stabbed after she was around the desk so she wouldn't have been close enough to the phone to reach it."

"The trail of evidence points to her being stabbed in-side but I think we may find that the person pursued her farther down the road, as it's hard to believe the note that was stuck on her back would have stayed there for any length of time." James shook his head. "Of course, depending on the rate the blood was seeping out her back, maybe it could have."

"I guess that will be something for you to try to recreate at the lab, won't it?" Maggie asked.

"Yes. That's on the agenda for sure." James smiled. "I think we're about done here, but we've been instructed to leave crime scene tape up for another day or so."

"Good plan," Jacob said. "We may need to come back as well."

The four of them walked out together with James being the last out. He locked the door and Angela put the tape over the entry so it could be determined later if someone had tampered with it.

Maggie led the way to the blue ATS Cadillac coupe parked beside the crime scene van. "I think this is our victim's car. Have you checked it out for any evidence?"

"No. It looks like it hasn't moved. Since we found a blood-drop trail—thin though it was—from her office across the grass to where she fell near the sidewalk, we didn't think we needed to," Angela said.

"Have it towed to the FDLE lab and check it out. You never know," Maggie said.

"Will do." James pulled a phone out of his pocket and used the voice command to dial the lab.

Before Maggie and Jacob could get in their own vehicle to drive to their next interview, Drusilla's husband stepped out of the passenger side of a black truck driven by another man.

He strode toward the Cadillac.

"What are you doing?" Jacob asked.

"Taking Dru's car home. These aren't cheap, and I can't leave it out here all night."

"We're impounding it," Maggie said.

"The woman is dead, and you're towing her car for parking too long?"

The look on Curtis Beane's face was so indignant, Maggie almost laughed.

"Of course not. We need to check it for evidence," James said.

"What kind of evidence you think you're gonna find in there?" Curtis jerked his head toward the car. "She was stabbed, shot, and strangled, wasn't she? Walked out of her office and down the street. Dru didn't get in that car since she parked it this morning."

Maggie nodded at Jacob. "You do the honors."

Jacob stepped forward and jangled his handcuffs. "We can do this the hard way or the easy way."

"What are you talking about? I'm here to get Dru's car."

"Not anymore. I'm taking you in for further questioning." Jacob took hold of Curtis's wrist and pulled it behind his back. "You have the right to remain si—"

"What'd I do? You didn't arrest me at my place. Why you 'resting me now?"

The man seemed genuinely confused.

"Let's just say you messed up." Maggie didn't want to give away yet what he said that led her and her partner—both experienced homicide detectives—to believe he had a hand in his wife's death.

CHAPTER 3

All the way to the station, Curtis whined and groaned about the unfairness of him being hauled there in cuffs. His carrying on was worse than any kid Maggie had ever heard.

After they arrived at their destination, Curtis kept up his litany of woe all the way across the parking lot and down the hallway to the interrogation room until Jacob kicked a chair toward him and said, "Sit."

The prisoner did as instructed but exhaled a huge puff of anger. "Can we at least take these off?" He lifted his arms.

Jacob removed the cuffs.

Curtis rubbed his wrists. "You didn't have to close them that tight. Where'd you think I was gonna go?"

At the table, Maggie took the seat across from Curtis while Jacob stood to one side, leaning on the wall with his arms crossed. She placed her note pad on the scarred wood surface. "Tell me how you knew your wife was shot?"

The information on the gunshot and poison hadn't been released to the media. His statement about it at the scene made him even more of suspect.

"Is that all? Me saying that got me arrested?" Curtis sniffed.

"You're not arrested, you're merely being detained," Jacob said.

"Let me say this, Cop. You put a man in cuffs, shove him in your car, and bring him to this place, you can call it whatever pretty name you want. I call it arrested."

"Just answer the question, please," Maggie said.

"Anne Leighton told me Dru was shot, stabbed, and strangled. She knew that and told me. No crime in that, is there? Last I heard, people are still allowed to talk in these here United States, ain't they?"

He had a point, and maybe Anne did know that or witnessed it. She would have to be questioned about Curtis's statement.

"Okay, let's say I believe you on that." Maggie made some notes on her pad then looked up. "How do you know Drusilla's car didn't move all day? Were you watching her?"

"Naw. No need. She hardly ever leaves her office once she goes to work. Other than to go outside to talk on her cell phone. She thinks Anne sometimes listens in on her personal calls, and she doesn't like that." Curtis grinned. "She might have wanted to listen to her assistant's calls once in a while. May have learned something."

"Like what?" Maggie pounced on his statement. What could he mean? "Did Anne have something to hide?"

The grin disappeared. "Nope. Nothing that I know of."

"Then what did you mean by that statement?" Jacob asked.

Curtis sat quietly for a moment—almost as if he was making up something to say—he finally responded, "Just that she was all about her. If she'd sometimes paid attention to other people, she may have been nicer to them."

"What a noble thought," Jacob said.

Maggie shook her head. "You still haven't answered my question. Do you have any personal knowledge that her car did *not* move today once she went in to work? Did you go to her office today?"

"Nope. Didn't go. Anne told me the car didn't move."

"Why would she tell you that?" Maggie asked.

"I called her and said I was going to get my pal to drive me over to pick it up and asked her about the keys."

"And she said…"

"That they were where Dru left them at eight-thirty this morning. She'd never left once she got there." The smug grin was back.

Maggie was almost positive he was lying. *Had* he been in the office that day? And more importantly, had he been one—or all—of her attackers?

Being unsure he was telling the truth and wanting to compare stories, Maggie stood and left the room. She hailed a uniformed officer to pay a visit to Ms. Leighton and bring her in for questioning.

When she returned, she addressed Jacob. "We have another witness coming in."

"What about me?" Curtis's whine had returned.

"You'll have to wait here a while. We'll bring you something to drink while you're alone."

Jacob followed her out.

They left Curtis in his interview room alone for the duration of Anne's interrogation. It never hurt to let a suspect sweat it out a little.

As soon as Anne was brought in, she was seated across from the two officers. She glared at Maggie and stuck her nose in the air.

Shaking her head at the gesture and the false bravado the lady was showing, Maggie said, "Nice to see you again, Anne. I hope things have been better for you since the last time we met."

"You have no right to drag me down here like a criminal. Who do you think you are?"

Maggie opened her notepad. "I'm the detective investigating the untimely death of your boss. I can bring in anyone I want."

"She wasn't just my boss, she was my friend." Anne practically spat the words at Maggie. "Everyone knows you hated Drusilla. You need to be removed from this case. She'll never get a fair deal with you doing the investigating."

"Hang on a minute here, lady," Jacob said. "Detective Blaine is one of the best cops in the state. She's going to do an excellent job on this case."

"Drusilla and this woman disliked each other. Why would Maggie even care who killed her?"

"It's my job to care. I can promise you we will look into every lead to find Drusilla's killer or killers. No matter what her history with me, I always do my job."

"Her history with *you*? Don't you mean after what you did to *her*?" Anne continued to address Maggie with a snippy tone.

"Maybe we need to agree to disagree about the way things ended with me and your boss. Let's just focus on trying to find justice for her."

"My *boss*, as you keep calling her, was my *friend.*" A sob escaped from all the anger directed at Maggie.

Maggie reached across the table to comfort the woman but pulled her hand back at the last moment.

They didn't have that kind of relationship, and Anne wouldn't welcome it anyway. And Maggie sure didn't want to have to tell this obviously distraught lady that her boss most certainly wasn't her friend. Sadly, Drusilla was a classic narcissist and couldn't really form a true attachment to anyone.

Jacob looked at Maggie. "How about getting our witness a cup of coffee or a soda?"

Getting the hint that Jacob thought he might get further in the interrogation without Maggie being present, she nodded. "Which would you prefer?" she asked Anne.

"Diet Coke." Just the two words, not a please or a thank you. Not that Maggie expected it from the woman who had formerly been at least a cordial acquaintance.

Leaving the room with no intention of bringing anyone anything to drink for a long while, Maggie turned the knob of the door next to the room she left.

Entering that one, she smiled at her boss and joined her at the two-way window to watch Jacob continue to question the witness.

"Nice try in there," Captain Bone said. "She's a tough dame, isn't she?"

"It's her putting on airs. She's been down and out. Drusilla helped her when she got divorced and had nowhere to live, so I think there's some deep gratitude there for that kindness."

"I heard the Isaacs woman never did anything out of kindness. Was this an aberration?"

"Maybe partially, but I think a lot of it was she needed someone at her office who wouldn't keep quitting. She couldn't keep staff, so if she let one live with her for a while, maybe loyalty would kick in."

Captain Bone raised her eyebrows. "I had no idea you were so cynical."

"I'm normally not. Unfortunately, I knew Drusilla Isaacs, and she truly was *not* a nice person." Maggie rubbed her hands on her thighs. "Don't get me wrong, she could put on the appearance of being sweet and kind. Even I was fooled for a long time. But then one day, you wake up and realize she's betrayed you."

"Was Ms. Leighton right? Are you all right on this case?"

"With all due respect, I think I am exactly the right person for this case since I have no delusions or illusions that the lady was a saint. I have a feeling this could get ugly before it's over."

"Uglier than stabbing, poisoning, shooting, and breaking a neck?"

"Sadly, yes." Maggie turned her attention to the window to see if Jacob was making any progress. "She had enemies spanning across the Florida panhandle all the way to the French Quarter in New Orleans, and those were only the ones I know about. There could very well be many more."

"How do you know these people you refer to as enemies?"

"Sadly, her reputation as someone who would be kind to your face and then jam it to you behind your back traveled around. Since she and I used to be friends and that was well-known, I would get calls often along the lines of 'what's wrong with Drusilla? She's such a jerk' and things like that. Some much stronger language as well. On what they called her, I mean."

"She sounds like she was always going to end up on Doc's slab with an unnatural cause of death. Let's see what Jacob is able to get out of her." Captain Bone faced the two-way glass again and turned up the volume on the speaker beside her.

"…you have no idea what he said then?" Jacob asked.

"Like I said, Drusilla's husband came in this morning irate about something to do with their gym membership. He was raving about the fact that Drusilla forgot to pay for his son's swimming lessons and he was embarrassed at the pool. That's all I heard before the door slammed shut. After that, they continued to speak in what sounded like anger, but it was hard to tell exactly what was said since the door was shut." Anne pushed her streaky hair back behind her ears.

Some women could pull off that look. Poor Anne looked like a zebra since clearly the person she hired to give her highlights flunked beauty school. If she hadn't been so snobby in the past, Maggie might have felt sorry for her, but it was hard to muster any pity.

One of Maggie's pet peeves was people who acted like they were better than others. Everyone was human and subject to making mistakes. No one should lord it over someone else. Shaking off her reverie about the witness, Maggie focused again on the conversation between Jacob and Anne.

"…they were in there for about thirty minutes."

"Did she eat or drink anything while he was there?" Jacob asked.

"Why would you want to know that? Wasn't she stabbed?" Anne leaned forward with her forearms on the scarred wooden table.

"I'm asking the questions. Did she eat or drink anything while Beane was there?"

Anne sat back hard in the chair, hands in her lap. "No. Not while he was there."

Maggie thought the witness was holding back. She was avoiding saying something. Silently urging Jacob to follow up, she found herself touching the glass.

Jacob asked what Maggie wanted to know. "So, she did after he left?"

"Yeah. Later in the morning, she drank one of those energy drinks she likes so much." Anne's face flushed and Maggie wondered what else the woman was hiding.

"And…" Jacob asked.

"And what?"

"Clearly, there's more to the story. I can tell from the way you're squirming in that chair."

Anne let out a little sigh. "All right. Yes, there's more. I was trying to protect her from people knowing, but I guess I better tell you."

"You should. It may help us figure out who killed her." Jacob tilted his chair back and placed his hands behind his head. It looked casual, but Maggie knew it meant he was ready to pay particular attention.

"Drusilla sometimes mixed Adderall with the energy drink. She said she liked the kick it gave her. If she didn't have the drug, she would use vodka, but she said it wasn't the same at all."

"Did she have a prescription?"

"No. Little Man did. She'd raid the bottle when he was with them."

"Little Man?" Jacob asked.

"Her husband's son. His name is Curtis Junior, and instead of calling him by the same name as his dad, they all call him Little Man."

"Poor kid. That must cause issues when they call roll at school."

"What's *that* supposed to mean? Do you think you're funny?" Anne flung her hair over her shoulder.

"No, not at all." The chair came down and landed on all four legs. "I merely was empathizing with a kid who isn't even allowed to have his own identity. Sadly, I've seen many with low or no self-worth choose the wrong path. If he hasn't got permission to use his name, I see issues in his future."

"Well, he's a cute kid, but I can't be worried about him."

"That seems kind of harsh, Miss Leighton."

She shrugged. "Can I go now? I don't know anything."

"You haven't told me yet where you were when you found out she was dead, and you haven't told us where you were at the time of her death."

"I was out of the office delivering some payroll tax returns when she died. When I came back, I saw all the police cars and an ambulance on the block where the office is. I couldn't get through so I parked and walked down the road toward the building."

"And then what happened? Did you find out it was Drusilla?"

"Yes. I saw her on the ground. Recognized her outfit." Anne looked as if she wanted to cry, but she didn't seem to be able to muster any tears.

"And instead of coming over and identifying yourself as her secretary, you fled the scene?"

"I certainly did not. There was a cop there who said I couldn't go into the building and needed to clear out of the way, so I went home. That was all." She tossed her hair over her shoulder yet again, causing Maggie to wonder if it was a nervous habit. "Besides, I probably would have been in more trouble if I ignored that policeman and walked right on back in the office, right? This is one of those situations where whatever I did, you'd be saying I was wrong. I'd bet my life on it."

Jacob shrugged. Maggie knew Anne was right about that. This was something they did in interrogation all the time. What she hadn't realized was Anne was that smart.

"Where's my drink Maggie was supposed to bring?" Anne looked around the room as if just realizing Maggie was gone.

"You mean Detective Blaine?"

"No, I mean Maggie. You forget, I've probably known her longer than you have. I call her Maggie."

"She's not your friend, is she?" Jacob leaned the chair back again.

"No, can't say she is or ever *has* been. She and Drusilla were close at one time, and I kind of liked her but once she and my boss split, I was loyal to Drusilla."

"What was the reason they split? Do you know?"

This was too much. Furious, Maggie turned away from the captain and the window. She snatched a soda from the mini-fridge on top of the table and stormed out of the viewing room and into the interrogation area where Jacob was trying to coax her secrets out of a witness—a woman she didn't like.

Stepping into the room, she addressed Anne. "Sorry it took so long. I couldn't find one that was already cold. Someone replenished the supplies but didn't put them in the fridge." Maggie slid it across the table.

"Thanks." Anne opened the flip-top and swigged down a big gulp.

Maggie sat. She glanced at Jacob and frowned, hoping he knew she was not happy with him at all. He'd overstepped and bad.

He merely stared at her as if he had nothing to be ashamed about.

"What about Curtis? Did he spend much time at the office today, Anne?" Maggie asked.

"Don't pretend you weren't listening in. I already told your partner here about Curtis coming and arguing with Drusilla."

"I wasn't listening. I was looking for your soda."

"Yeah, right." Anne took another swallow. "Can I leave now? Am I under arrest?"

"No. You're free to go for now since it's getting late, but I want you to think back over the last few days and make us a list of everyone who came in to see her at work. Phone numbers and addresses. By tomorrow, please." Maggie stood and walked to the door. "We'll come by your place for it in the morning. The crime scene tape will be up for a couple more days."

"What's going to happen to my job?" Anne rose.

"I don't know. I guess you'll have to send out some resumes. I sincerely hope you find something soon. This is tough, I'm sure," Maggie said.

"Like you really care." Anne pivoted on her heel and strode down the hall.

Maggie caught up to her. "Listen. I never had any personal animosity toward you. I don't know where you got that from, but I don't wish you ill. I also didn't wish this for Drusilla."

"You go on and tell yourself that all you want." Anne marched out of the station, leaving Maggie, in disbelief at the venom in the woman's voice, in her wake.

☙❧

When she recovered herself, Maggie returned to the interrogation room. "Have someone go check all the dumpsters around Drusilla's office, and if they've already been taken to the dump, send someone to that section. We need to find that can of energy drink and see what else might be in it. That could very well be the way the poison was ingested."

Captain Bone nodded. "I'm sure the CSIs collected the trash in the office but now that we know our victim liked to mix prescription drugs with energy drinks and the poison question is there, good idea to check the surrounding area in case whoever we're looking for got rid of the evidence further afield."

"I'm starting to like Miss Leighton for at least the poisoning part," Maggie said.

Why's that?" Jacob asked. "I thought she was all about being Drusilla's friend and assistant."

"There's just something about her. I can't put my finger on it at the moment, but when you interviewed her, some word, some nuance, or…man, I just can't place it yet, but there was something that was off."

"Here we go again with one of your hunches, Mags. What do you think it was?" Jacob asked.

"Like I said, I've got no idea right now, but it'll click. It always does." Maggie poured herself a cup of coffee. "Is it almost time to go home? I feel like we've been here forever."

"It has been a long day. You should both go home and start fresh in the morning," Captain Bone said.

"We have more witnesses to interview." Maggie gulped some of her coffee so fast, she scalded her tongue.

"They'll be there tomorrow. We'll probably have more as well once all the patrol officers come in with their notes from the area canvass. I insist you both go." The captain laughed. "If it makes you feel any better, I can order you to return at six a.m."

"Oh, please, not that. Maggie knows how I need my sleep. She'd never agree to us coming in before shift starts." Jacob opened the door. "I'm getting out of here before I find myself on call for four a.m."

Maggie shook her head as she followed him down the hall. She didn't know what he was going on about. Many a time they'd both come in at ungodly hours. Homicides waited for no man.

She was glad to be allowed to go home, though. It

had been a rough shift. Seeing Drusilla dead was a shock to her system, and she knew she needed some time to process it. Now they would never have a chance to try to make things right between them.

Being a hardnosed cop wasn't a natural state for Maggie. She hid a soft heart under her brusque, capable exterior. She was fully aware of it since she'd been doing it all her life.

As she drove the short distance to her house, she lectured herself. "You *have* to do this. You can set aside the past and let it go. Now that she's gone, there's no need to hang on to the hurt. She deserves justice like everyone else. Just because she treated people like they were disposable doesn't mean she herself was. No one should be hated enough for the kind of end she met."

Turning the radio on to drown out her own words, Maggie tried to sing along to the oldie playing. She failed miserably as her overactive brain kept circling back to Drusilla and how she looked there on the ground. Maggie didn't know how she would ever be able to get it out of her head and sleep.

When she pulled into her driveway, she wasn't surprised to see Jacob's car already at her house.

Getting out, she shut her car door.

Jacob met her at the door. "Sorry. I know this is getting old, but maybe someday, I can go home and spend a whole night there again."

"Hey, you know my spare room is always open. I

have no idea why you won't use the key I gave you but you're completely welcome to stay here as long as you want or need to."

"You know I appreciate it. I don't use the key because I don't want to start to act like this is really my place." He grinned. "Besides, some day, you may actually want to bring a man home, and if I'm already here and in my bed, that may chase your potential lover away."

"*Please*. That's not going to happen. I haven't met anyone I'd even consider bringing home with me in a very long time." She opened the door and tossed her keys on the foyer table as he followed her inside.

"What about that lawyer you said asked you out after you were in the courthouse testifying the other day?"

"Like I told you then, I turned him down. Sure, he's cute, but I've heard he's a player, and I'm not interested in that kind of thing. Besides, what would we talk about? I put people away. He keeps them out of jail. Not a good combination for a smooth relationship."

"You don't even give a guy a chance before you reject him." Jacob went to the kitchen and poured himself a glass of water from the tap.

"Nope. Not anymore. I seem to always find some reason either not to go out with them or something wrong once I do. I'm aware of the issue and also why I do it but don't let it worry you. Someday, I'll get past it and surprise you with an awesome guy you won't believe would ever be attracted to me."

"I hope that's true. I really do. You deserve to be happy again."

"As do you, my friend." Maggie sent a small smile in his direction. She truly did wish he could be happy and content again. And to be able to face the demons that seemed to wait for him at his house.

"I'm turning in. See you in the morning." Jacob neatly avoided responding to her well wishes for him and turned toward the spare bedroom.

Maggie took a quick shower to try to lose the grime of the day and went to bed.

Her last thoughts as she fell off to sleep were of Drusilla's dead body on the sidewalk, still with just one stiletto on and lime green toenails on the bare foot. But this time, she was sitting up, breast still hanging out of her blouse, and holding a can of energy drink.

CHAPTER 4

The next day after stopping for breakfast at Waffle House, Maggie and Jacob returned to the tedious task of interviewing witnesses. The captain had been right. There were a number of other people who gave short statements to the uniformed officers. Most of them could be sorted through and added to the murder book without an urgent need to speak again to that particular person.

There were a couple that did need a follow up visit. One was Drusilla's former husband, and another was a neighbor from the apartment complex across the street from where the victim fell.

They decided to hit the apartment complex first. "Come on. Let's hope this guy isn't a nine-to-five worker and is at home right now," Maggie said as she walked up the stairs to the second floor outer hallway to the apartments.

Jacob followed her to the door they were seeking. "I think he's home. Notes say he works at a food mart. No telling when his shift is, though."

A man who appeared to be in his late sixties answered their knock. He nodded at their badges. "Figured someone with some authority would be back. Might as well come on in." He stepped aside to let them enter. "I'm John Hayes."

Maggie glanced around the tiny living room. It seemed their witness had served some time in the military. On every wall and surface was either some patriotic poster, a flag, or some item from an exotic place. She recognized some expensive Japanese ceramics and some butter jade from Africa.

To break the ice, she asked, "What branch did you serve in?"

"Navy. Thirty years."

"That's wonderful. I bet you got to see some interesting things over the years." Maggie took a seat in the easy chair he indicated that was opposite to the one he took.

"I have. But nothing like that scene I saw with that poor woman out there yesterday." He tilted his head toward the window.

Jacob still stood, leaning against the doorjamb with his ankles crossed. "That's what we want to ask you about. We know you talked to a uniformed officer, but we'd like you to tell us again—and more importantly—show us where you were when you saw what you witnessed."

Mr. Hayes placed his hands on his knees and seemed to use that as leverage to be able to pull himself out of the chair. He walked over to the large window that looked out over the crime scene. Placing his index finger on the plate glass, he pointed down to the ground. "I was in my chair over there and heard what sounded like an argument outside. I figured it must have been some kind of fight, since it was loud enough for me to hear over the TV."

Maggie wondered if it had taken him as long to stand then as it had just taken but didn't want to ask yet. She nodded her encouragement for him to go on.

"When I got over here, I could see that woman who died. There was a man with her, and they were screaming at each other."

"What time was it, and could you tell if she was hurt?" Jacob asked.

"It was early in the day." Mr. Hayes laughed. "She might have been having some hurt feelings, but she was right as rain physically."

Maggie came to stand beside him so she could tell how far it was and how well someone could actually see what was happening on the ground. "How could you tell?"

"She wasn't all bloody like she was when she was

found, and she was pretty agile when she launched herself at the man she was arguing with."

"Launched?" Maggie asked.

"Sure did. She threw herself at him and started banging away on his chest, screeching all the while."

Jacob stepped over as well. "What was she saying?"

"I couldn't hear it all, but she seemed upset that the man had some kids, and she didn't."

"What exactly did you hear?" Maggie was getting a bit anxious that Hayes would never tell them what he heard. Was he also lonely like poor Hattie Simpkins and wanted someone to be a companion? Was that why he was dragging this out?

"I can't quote the exact words, but I heard words about marriage, divorce, left her because didn't he want children, and then it seems like the guy has a couple of kids now—that aren't hers. I figure the two of them were married at some time and got a divorce because he didn't want any kids, and now he's got some. She wasn't happy about that turn of events." Mr. Hayes moved away from the window. "They both left after that, and it was a few hours later that I saw the woman out there dead."

"Did you hear anything at all between when they left and when you saw her dead?" Jacob asked.

"No. I had the TV on and was watching some programs. I didn't hear another peep until I heard the police out there." He shrugged. "I may have dozed off. I tend to do that when I sit for too long. Getting old isn't fun."

"Can you describe the man you saw out there arguing with her?" Maggie asked.

"Tall, dark-haired. White. Maybe in his early thirties."

It sounded to Maggie as if Hayes was describing Drusilla's former husband, David. She knew they'd divorced several years ago because she wanted to try to have a child and he didn't. He'd quit coming home for a number of months. Then one day, he showed up with divorce papers. Maggie hadn't heard he was now a father.

Since he was their next stop, she made a mental note to ask about any children he had.

Jacob handed Mr. Hayes one of his cards. "Call us if you think of anything else. Try to remember exactly what you heard if you can and write it down. It could help us a lot."

"I don't think that guy she was with when I saw her did it."

"Why?" Maggie asked.

"Well, the way I figure it, if he was gonna take her out, he'd have done it then. I mean, the lady was all over him. Acting like a lunatic."

Jacob flipped his notebook closed. "Maybe he came back later when he could do it more quietly. If he'd done it then, there would probably have been witnesses since it sounds as if the whole neighborhood would've been able to hear them."

"You might have a point there…" Mr. Hayes looked

down at the card in his hand. "…Detective Brown."

Jacob nodded. "Come along, Blaine. Time to make a visit to our next witness."

Maggie shook Mr. Hayes's hand. "Do you happen to know the lady who lives across the road over there in that little blue house?"

"No. Can't say that I do. I kind of keep to myself over here." He tilted his head as if curious. "Why do you ask?"

"I met her yesterday. She's a kind soul and since you are as well, I thought perhaps the two of you were acquainted. Living so near to each other, that is."

Mr. Hayes's smile transformed his face. "That's so nice of you to say. I appreciate the compliment."

"I'm planning to go over to see her on Saturday. Perhaps you'd like to come as well?"

Hayes looked a bit surprised but nodded. "That would be nice. I'd be happy to come."

"Then I'll call you with the time as soon as I know it." Maggie opened the door. "We'll see you later."

As they walked down the stairway, Jacob said, "What are you doing? Playing matchmaker?"

"Not at all. It just occurred to me that the lonely lady who lives alone with her cat and the navy veteran who spends his days watching TV and working at a convenience store might enjoy having someone to chat with once in a while. They live so close, there's no need for them to each be alone all the time."

He shook his head as he led the way to the car. "Never thought I'd see the day."

"What?"

"That you were so sentimental."

Maggie grinned. "I have depths you have no idea about."

"I'm beginning to see that, partner."

⁊

They pulled up in front of the gym where David Isaacs worked as the manager. When he and Drusilla divorced, she kept his last name, as that was the name she had on her office and CPA certificate. She didn't want any confusion or loss of client referrals by the change in name.

Maggie never understood that. If the man she loved came home one day and said he didn't want her or to have children with her, she would've shed his name in a heartbeat, career or no career.

They entered the gym. Maggie glanced around for David. She knew him vaguely from when she and Drusilla were friends. Only by sight, though. She'd never had a conversation with the man.

She spied him with a female customer assisting her on the weight machine, his left hand on her breast. Maggie wondered how he was explaining to the lady the need to grab her boob in order to help her clang the bars together to work her upper body.

"I've never seen a guy feel up a chick to set the weights on that machine," Jacob said.

"That's why I like you, partner."

"Why?"

"We think alike." She paused. "Sometimes."

"I'm thinking the dude is a breast man. His ex-wife had a set of knockers and so does the current woman he's pawing."

"She doesn't seem to mind, but let's go relieve her of his presence." Maggie led the way across the room. She showed her badge on her hip to David. "I'm Detective Blaine, and this is my partner, Detective Brown. We have a few questions for you about Drusilla."

"Can't you see I'm working? I don't have time for this." David poked his bottom lip out like a little kid who was told he couldn't have a turn on the merry-go-round.

"We hate to take you away from such a pleasant task, but you can give us five minutes here, or we can haul you down to the station," Jacob said. "Which will look better to your staff and customers? I'm easy. Either one works for me."

"I divorced that evil bitch. Why should I be questioned? I haven't even seen her."

For the moment, Maggie ignored the apparent lie since they couldn't be sure David was who Mr. Hayes saw until they could do a lineup. "That's why we need to talk."

"What do you mean by that?" David placed his hands on his hips and stood with his legs apart. Kind of an unconscious superman look. Without the cape, of course.

"The fact that you still have so much animosity toward her places you squarely into the camp of people we need to talk to," Maggie said.

"Yeah, man, if you wanted to be left alone, you should've manufactured some tears and expressed your deep sorrow at her loss," Jacob said.

The woman sitting at the machine stood abruptly and scurried off.

"Look what you did. You chased off that new member. What if she doesn't sign up for the year contract after her three free sessions?"

"Can't blame us. We asked you to step aside to chat. You chose to mouth off instead. For all you know, that chick thinks you're a murderer and is off to tell everyone in the locker room." Jacob pulled out his cuffs. "We better take you in before you cost the place more business."

David threw his hands up in surrender. "No, no. That won't be necessary. Come to my office."

Jacob looked at Maggie as if for permission.

She shrugged. "Fine for now, but keep those cuffs handy, Detective." She had no doubt they'd convinced David it was in his interest to talk to them, but she didn't want to lose the advantage by letting him think he was safe. Besides, they still might need that lineup.

Once they were seated in David's cubicle, Jacob opened his notepad and asked, "Do you know anyone who would want Drusilla dead?"

"Like I told you, I haven't seen her, but I *can* say this." David rubbed the side of his nose. "Last I heard, there was no one who wanted her alive." He snickered.

"That's not a very nice thing to say about anyone," Maggie said.

"Can't help it if it's the truth. That woman could make anyone want to slit her throat." He tilted his head. "Hey, I remember Drusilla had a friend with the last name Blaine. She was a cop. Was that you?"

Maggie hesitated for a moment then decided it didn't matter if he knew she was that same cop. After all, what could he do? He wasn't the next of kin. He couldn't have her removed from the investigation. "Yes, that was me, but we're asking the questions here."

"Just making a point, Detective. You knew her. Obviously, you know how terrible she could be. She treated everyone like crap and then put on that fake face, wondering why everyone was mad at her. If anyone can understand the need to strangle my ex, it would be some-one who'd been around her a lot. Like you."

"Interesting that you used the word strangled," Jacob said.

"Yeah, I know she was strangled. Everyone in town

heard. But I also said 'slit her throat,' and I don't think that happened, did it?"

"That's true, so let's change the topic." Maggie leaned forward. "Where were you yesterday in the morning?"

"Here. I came in at eight and didn't leave until four."

"No lunch hour?" Maggie asked.

David smirked. "Ate a banana and had a smoothie."

Maggie wanted to try to catch him off guard to see if he would admit to being on the street with her. "Did you and Drusilla ever talk about having children?"

He shook his head. "Nope, can't say that we did. What's that got to do with her dying?"

"Why did you get divorced?" Jacob asked.

"Just couldn't stand her anymore. I had to get out." David pushed his chair back and stood. "I really need to get back to work now."

"We're not quite through." Jacob made a note on his pad. "Did you remarry and do you have any children with your current wife?"

"This really is too much. My personal life is not your business. If you think I had something to do with Drusilla's death, arrest me now or get out of here." The index finger he pointed at the door had a distinct shake to it.

Unsure if his anger was because he thought they were prying too much into his business or if it was because they hit close on the underlying issue of his marriage to Drusilla, Maggie decided to play the line-up card.

She rose from the cheap office chair she'd been sitting in. "Fine. We're not quite ready to arrest you yet, but we do need you to come down to the station for a lineup."

David's face paled. "Why? Because I won't tell you about my new wife and kids? Isn't that some kind of police brutality?"

"Not at all, but thanks for verifying you are married and have children," Maggie said. She looked down at her watch then back up at Mr. Isaacs. "You have one hour. That's how long it'll take us to get the lineup set. If you don't show, we *will be* back for you. This is your chance to walk out of here without embarrassment. If we have to come back, it won't be pretty." Maggie turned to the door. "Let's go."

Jacob followed her. Over his shoulder, he said, "Remember, one hour."

Once they were out in the street, Jacob said, "Why would he lie about seeing her unless he had something to do with it? He had to know someone would have heard that argument. It wasn't like they were trying to keep quiet. She was practically accosting him in the street according to Hayes."

"I think he's just an idiot. He seems a bit too stupid to pull off any kind of complicated plot. If he did anything, he's the one who stabbed her or poisoned her. Stabbings are way more personal than shootings, and I think he'd have done whatever he did in private. The other elements were more public. I see this guy as a closet lurker."

Jacob laughed as he opened the driver's side door. "What exactly is a closet lurker?"

"A person who does ugly deeds behind closed doors and acts like a prince in public."

"Don't forget that dude was groping a client in full view of the whole gym he manages. He's not a prince by any meaning of the word."

CHAPTER 5

The lineup started at eleven. They'd rounded up a number of men of the same approximate weight and height as David Isaacs. Some had lighter hair color and some the same or slightly darker. Three of the men were cops.

Before they brought in Mr. Hayes, one of the patrolmen who'd been recruited to be a suspect on the lineup said, "What if the dude IDs me?"

Captain Bone laughed. "You got something to confess, Roberts?"

"No, but has that ever happened? The witness picked one of the plants?" Roberts asked.

"Not while I've been around, but I'm sure it has probably happened somewhere in the world." The captain nodded at the three officers. "Go on now, we're ready to bring you all in, and, once you're in place, we'll show in the witness." She grinned at Roberts. "Try not to look so nervous."

While they were settling into place, Maggie went down the hall to get Mr. Hayes from the room where they'd been holding him in seclusion so he wouldn't see anyone, and the lineup wouldn't be tainted.

"How does this work?" he asked her as they strolled down the corridor.

"We'll go in, and a curtain will be opened with several people behind it. They won't be able to see you as they're behind one-way glass. Each will have a number, and you'll look them over. If you want anyone to move forward for a closer look or you want them to say anything, let me know, and we'll arrange that as well."

"You sure they can't see me?"

"Positive."

"What if I pick one? Does he get arrested or will he be freed and know it was me that said it was him out there with that woman?"

They arrived at the door and stopped outside it as Maggie reached for the door knob. "Chances are, he won't be arrested as we don't really have enough to hold him on a murder charge, but we will be very interested in questioning him some more. You'll be given a ride home and will be there before he's let out of here. If our questioning results in enough to arrest him, we will. Immediately." She pulled on the door but didn't open it. "You ready?"

He nodded. "As ready as I'll ever be. I'm not sure I've been this nervous since I left 'Nam."

"It's going to be fine. I promise."

Inside the room was Maggie, Mr. Hayes, Captain Bone, Jacob, and a lawyer that David Isaacs brought with him.

The captain addressed Hayes. "Ready?"

He nodded, and the curtain opened.

Hayes took his time and walked the length of the line, peering at each man in turn. He turned and walked past them again before saying, "It's number four."

"Didn't you want to ask them to say anything?" Jacob asked.

"Nope, I'm sure it's number four."

"You can't be too sure." The lawyer stepped over to Hayes as if to intimidate him. "You walked back and forth and stared pretty hard at each one of them before you said a word. How can you expect us to trust your identification? Surely, if you saw the man at all with the victim, you'd have recognized him immediately."

Not backing down, Hayes stared the man in the eyes. "I *did* know him as soon as the curtain opened, but I figured if I said it too quickly, you'd be all over me for jumping too fast. You lawyers are all alike. A mere human can never satisfy you." He nodded curtly. "It's him. That's the guy I saw out my window. I guess he's your client or you wouldn't be trying to get me to change my mind."

The lawyer let out a snort and turned to the captain. "Just because this man says he saw my client with the victim doesn't make my guy a murderer."

"No, it doesn't, but it does open him up to some additional questioning since he lied to my detectives." Captain Bone shook Mr. Hayes's hand. "A patrolman will take you home. Thank you for coming in."

"I want to make sure his lawyer doesn't get to tell that guy I was the one to point him out. I don't want any trouble."

"He won't. Because if you do have any issues, you call me, and I'll have it taken care of," Captain Bone said. She looked at the lawyer, "Right?"

"Yes, ma'am. We know how this works. We only disclose this witness's name if my guy is charged and this man becomes an active witness in the case."

Hayes left the room. Maggie looked at the lawyer. "I presume you want to be in on this round of questioning?"

"Absolutely."

"Let's head down the hall then while the captain takes care of disbanding the lineup." Maggie led the way to the interview room.

When they were seated and David Isaacs joined them, Maggie said, "Now, do you want to tell us exactly when was the last time you saw your former wife? Or do you want to stick to that same story you told earlier about not seeing her in a long time?"

Isaacs let out a massive sigh. "Do I really have to do that? You know your witness just said it was me arguing with the bitch the other day."

"So, you *are* changing your story?" Jacob asked as he jotted something in his notebook.

"Yeah, of course, I am. I'm sure your witness is some kind of saint who would never not tell the truth, so yes, you got me. I was there, but she was alive and fine when I left. As bitchy and mean as she ever was." Isaacs ran his hand over his brow. "Believe me, if I was ever going to kill that woman it would've been when we were married and I couldn't get away from her. Now that I'm not shackled to her any longer, she could've lived to a hundred as far as I'm concerned. As long as she left me alone."

"Why were you there?" Maggie asked. "If you wanted her to leave you alone, why were you bothering her?"

Isaacs held his hands up. "Now, now, I wasn't bothering her. She's the one who called me, all in an uproar about her mortgage."

"Her mortgage? On her house or her office?" Jacob asked.

"She doesn't own that office, man. She pays a lot of rent for that place from some old lawyer up on Main Street. Pretends it's hers to show off and act like she's more successful than she is, but it ain't hers."

"Couldn't anyone check that at the property office?" Maggie asked then shook her head. What did that matter? "Never mind. Let's talk about her house mortgage then. Why was she calling you about that?"

He looked a bit sheepish and glanced over at his lawyer before answering. "I was supposed to get my name off it. She arranged to refinance, but I never seemed to find the time to go sign the paperwork. It's just one more hassle I don't have time for."

"And so, she called you and asked you to do it, and what happened from there?" Maggie asked.

"She demanded I come over to her office and ride with her to the bank. When I got there, she was outside talking on that infernal cell phone she always has in her hand. I pulled over when I saw her on the sidewalk."

"And then what happened?" Maggie nodded her encouragement.

"I parked, got out, and asked her to put the phone down so we could go take care of this, and I could get back to my business." He put his hands on the tabletop and ran them back and forth on the surface. "She hung up and then started pounding me on the chest, yelling about me having two kids with my new wife and not knowing how that hurt her and not knowing when to stop and how much she hated me for taking that away from her."

"Not knowing when to quit?" Jacob asked. "What's that supposed to mean?"

"Isn't it obvious?" Isaacs asked with a smirk.

"Not to us. How about enlightening us?" Jacob said as he looked over at Maggie who shook her head.

The lawyer interjected, "Maybe you and I need to chat about this first, David. I don't know what you're going to say and thus can't advise you on whether you should speak."

Isaacs patted his lawyer's hand on the table. "It's okay. They can't do anything about this." With a gloating look on his face, he said, "My new wife—the improvement on the old one—is pregnant with number three. Drusilla had just taken a call from someone who told her as I was driving over. So, she was already mad at me about the mortgage and then she was mad about the new kid."

"Why would she still care that you were having kids with someone else? Isn't she remarried, too?" Maggie really was confused about that. There was clearly a lot she didn't understand about Drusilla Isaacs.

"She can't have kids." David Isaacs let out a bitter little laugh. "Well, of course, she's dead now and can't, but what I meant was, she lost her chance to have a kid when we broke up."

"How's that? Only your sperm could impregnate her?" Jacob asked.

"Of course not. The woman had endometriosis and had several surgeries trying to fix it. Her best shot was when she was younger. Once she hit about twenty-eight, her chances went down. Eventually, she was infertile.

Blamed me for not getting her pregnant while we were together. Then, of course, my new girl got pregnant before we were even married. Drusilla never forgave me." He shrugged. "But lord knows, she would've been a terrible mother. She's so self-centered, the poor kid wouldn't have had a chance."

Maggie didn't want to think about what chance this man's kids had since he seemed a bit shallow and egotistical himself. Of course, she *did* know Drusilla and wondered how she would have actually done with a child.

"And that was what the fight was about?" Jacob asked.

"Yep. That was it. She made me so mad punching me in the chest that I refused to go to the bank with her. I got back in my car once I could get her off me, and then I left."

"Did you see her again after that?" Maggie asked.

He shook his head. "Nope. Sure didn't."

"How can we trust you when we know you already lied to us?" Jacob asked.

"When I left Drusilla, I went to the gym and didn't leave until it closed that night at ten. I was seen by all kinds of members, and you can also check out the cameras inside the club and see me on there."

"What about your wife?" Maggie threw the question out there to see if she got a reaction.

A red flush worked its way up Isaacs' neck. "What about her?"

"Where was she when all this was happening?"

"At home. With our two kids."

Maggie kept up the pressure. "And you know this how? If you were at work?"

"Because she doesn't have a car when I'm not there for her to use mine or for me to take her places."

"How do you know she didn't borrow a car?"

David Isaacs leapt from his chair and lunged for Maggie in almost the same movement.

Jacob stood and stepped toward Isaacs coming between him and the edge of the table. "I suggest you back off, Isaacs. You *are* in a police station, you know."

"She's got no right to suggest my wife had anything to do with Drusilla's death. No right at all." Isaacs was on the verge of tears.

His lawyer took him by the arm. "I think this interview is over. If you have something to charge my client with, do it, or we're leaving."

Jacob jerked his head toward the door. "Go on then, but don't think you're in the clear. Just because we have nothing to hold you on doesn't mean we're writing you off as a suspect."

As soon as they were out of the room, Jacob addressed Maggie, "What was *that* all about?"

"Proving the man can be volatile himself and not merely be responding to Drusilla's outburst. The man is clearly capable of violence. You saw how he came at me."

"Defending his woman's honor, though, Mags. Not just being violent for violence's sake."

"Still. It's something."

☙☙☙

Later that day, a call came into the precinct and was routed to Maggie. When she picked up, a man with a raspy voice said, "I saw you're the detective on that murder case. I want to report something. About that dead woman accountant."

"What's your name?" Maggie asked.

"You don't need to know that. Police take anonymous tips all the time."

She wasn't going to tell him they would be able to trace the call. Let him talk now, and she'd find out where he was later. Of course, if he'd watched even one TV show in the last ten years, he had to know they could trace him, but if he wanted to pretend he was anonymous, she'd go along with that. "You're right. What's the info you have?"

"I found a gun."

Now, this *was* news. Maggie snapped her fingers to get Jacob's attention so he could listen in.

Holding the phone away from her ear, she said, "I hope you haven't touched it. We'll need to get prints off it. Can you tell me where you found it?"

"There won't be any prints. It was in the water under the pier. It's full of salt water. I doubt you can even fire it."

"What makes you think it's related to the murder of Drusilla Isaacs? She was killed downtown and nowhere near the beach."

"I happen to know it's her own gun. She may not have been killed with it, but since it belongs to her, I thought I'd call you. If you don't want it, that's fine. I'll hang up now and keep it for myself."

"Wait a minute. How do you know it's hers? A gun is a gun, isn't it? How do you tell by looking at it that it belongs to a certain person unless you happen to know the serial number?" It dawned on Maggie that this caller may have been close enough to Drusilla to have that information. Was this the person who shot her and was the raspy quality of the voice an attempt to disguise it?

The caller laughed. "No, I don't know the serial number."

"Then how do you know it's hers?"

"It's pink and has her initials in some kind of crystals on it."

Stunned at the craziness of a gun being blinged out as well as pink, for a second Maggie didn't know how to respond. Finally, she asked, "Where can I pick it up?"

"Oh, so you *do* want it?" The man laughed again, sounding as if he were a three pack a day smoker for at least twenty years.

"Yes, we do. Let's set a time and place for me to re-trieve it. If you could, I'd like you to put in in in a baggie so we can be sure that the lab can get what it can out of it."

"I can do that, but like I said, I don't think they're going to get much. It's sandy, and I bet saltwater is all in the barrel."

"Are you still under the pier? Can I come there for it?"

"Oh, no. I've left there. I'm at one of the only pay phones left on the planet. The parking lot of the Walmart on Gulf Breeze Parkway."

Maggie nodded to Jacob who took off to make a call to a patrol car to get to that Walmart. She knew he'd have to also call the county sheriff on that side of the bridge since it was not their jurisdiction. She was determined to keep the man on the line until someone could get there.

"I didn't know there was a pay phone there. I thought they were all gone."

"Nope. And I don't believe that you didn't know it. I think you're trying to keep me on the phone."

With that, the man hung up.

Furious, Maggie slammed down the receiver. "Damn."

"You think that was something more than a prank call?" Jacob was back. He leaned his hip on the side of her desk. "I'd bet a T-bone steak it was a hoax."

"I don't know. It kind of rang true to me."

"A pink gun with crystals? That sounds like something a Power Ranger would have." Jacob snickered. "Just let it go. We have some other statements to go through and should have some results from the crime scene lab folks soon. Besides, if the gun really existed and it was in the shape this guy says, I bet it would be worthless as evidence, anyway. So, forget it and let's focus on what we *do* have."

Maggie still thought the man on the phone was legit, but Jacob was right. There was nothing she could do about it now. If only they'd been quicker with that call to the neighboring county.

She shuffled through some of the papers on her desk. "Somewhere in here is a report on the kind of blade Doc said was used to stab Drusilla. It was some type of hunting knife. I thought maybe we could check around and see if it's rare or something that can be bought anywhere."

"I'm sure it's probably standard issue. Rare knives are rare."

"Ha, ha. Very cute. I'm trying to find something to move forward with, and you're making jokes."

Jacob reached over and moved the pile of folders. "Come on."

"What? Where?"

"Just come with me." He stood and walked out of the bullpen area, acting as if he knew she would follow along immediately.

She shrugged and got up. Might as well see what he was going to do.

When they arrived at the parking lot, he unlocked his car and pointed at the passenger door. "Get in."

"Where are we going?"

"You'll see." He drove toward the mall and pulled into the parking lot of the Marble Slab Creamery.

"What's this?" Maggie looked askance at him.

"You needed a break and what's better than ice cream? Haven't you always said chocolate makes everything better?"

"Yeah, but I don't think I ever said chocolate ice cream."

"I took the liberty of adding the ice cream part because that's my weakness. I figured we'd feed both our vices at once."

"Might as well indulge since we're here." Maggie opened her door, surprised at how pleased she was at being taken out of the station for a moment of pure pleasure. She didn't often allow herself to get distracted when she was on a case, but this felt right for some reason.

Inside the creamery, Jacob added so many ingredients to his concoction, she shook her head. "Is there any ice cream in there at all, or is it all toppings?"

He tapped his spoon on her cup. "Tend to your own, Detective."

They sat outside and enjoyed the sunshine while they ate.

A woman with purple-dyed hair came out with a cup of ice cream. She stopped at Maggie and Jacob's table. "Did I hear you call her 'detective,' sir?" the woman asked.

"Yes. I did. We're both detectives. Do you need to report a crime?" Jacob smiled. He could usually put people at ease with his mild manner.

"I'm not sure. I heard about that accountant lady that was killed, and I might have something to say to whoever is in charge of that."

This was too weird. What were the odds of there being a witness at this place at the same time as them? Maggie knew them to be astronomical. It had to be some kind of gag. She stood. "We need to go."

"Wait a sec, Mags. This is legit. I know you won't believe it, but I spoke to a woman on the phone earlier and arranged to meet her here. It was the plan to get you in a better mood as well as meet with a potential witness." He glanced up at the girl and back at Maggie. "This must be her."

"Yes, that was me," the girl said. "I called in because I heard a guy talking on the phone about a gun and then he hung up and darted to the parking lot. He got into a black Plymouth Charger. I wrote down the tag number to call it in. I was afraid he might be some kind of criminal out to hurt someone."

"Why didn't you just call in to a dispatcher and give the number?" Maggie asked.

"I was scared. He saw me as I was waiting to use the phone because the battery was dead on mine. I figured I'd meet with an officer and give it over that way. You know, in exchange for some kind of protection if the guy comes after me."

Maggie thought it all sounded unbelievable and unreliable, but then she remembered her gut feeling about the man on the phone being on the up and up, so she stayed seated and continued to eat her ice cream. "What's the tag info?"

The girl gave the number, and Jacob called it in.

After taking a formal statement from the girl, including her name and address, Jacob let her go with a promise that he'd arrange for extra drive-bys on her street by the police department for the next few nights.

Almost as soon as she was gone, the dispatcher rang back with the information on the driver.

Jacob tossed his cup and spoon in the trash. "Ready to roll? We have a couple of uniforms meeting us at the address on the car's registration."

"Then let's go." Maggie threw away her container as well and followed Jacob to his car.

She wondered exactly who and what they would find there—and if she was about to come face to face with at least one of the people who played a part in the death of Drusilla.

CHAPTER 6

They drove across town and ended up in a sketchy neighborhood. The house had definitely seen better days. The green paint was peeling, and the shutters were hanging askew. There was no grass in the yard, but it was clear someone had once lived there who cared about the property since there were signs of some old azaleas and dogwood trees that were neglected and ratty looking now but would have been beautiful at some point.

"Nice place, huh?" Jacob said as he got out and stared at the home with hands on his hips.

Maggie placed her hand on the butt of her gun. "Hopefully, the inside is better than the out."

Two marked cars pulled up, and four officers got out. "What's the plan?" the oldest officer asked.

"How about the two of you cover the back?" Jacob tilted his head at the first officer. He turned to the other two. "And you cover Detective Blaine on the porch. I'll stand to her side where I can't be seen in case we need to move in fast."

They all nodded and moved into place.

Maggie stepped up onto the small, rickety porch and rang the bell.

It echoed through the house as if the place was empty.

They all looked at each other and Jacob shrugged. "No one home. I guess we'll need a stake out."

Before anyone could react, a scuffle at the side of the house caught Maggie's attention. "Hurry, it sounds like our guy could be on the run."

The two uniformed officers and Maggie headed around the home and left Jacob in the front.

As they came around the corner, one of the two officers from the back of the house called out, "Stop right there."

The other officer was pursuing the runner, and just as the word "there" was said, the officer lunged and grabbed their escapee by the leg of his trousers. The runner fell hard and flat on his chest, letting out an "oof" as he landed.

The officer cuffed the man and left him on the ground. Maggie dashed over and helped him sit up but held her hand out for the man to stay on the ground. "Are you the person who called the police station and gave information to us about Drusilla Isaacs's gun?"

"How did you find me?" He practically spat the words.

"Funny thing about that. There was a witness. Got us your tag number. And you weren't in Gulf Breeze, you were by the mall when you called." Maggie loomed over the man and glared at him, hoping to intimidate him into being cooperative. "The registration to that car says it belongs to a Linus Anthony. Is that you? Or do we have a stolen car on our hands?"

"Are you stupid, Detective?" he asked. "If I was in that house that the car registration is attached to, wouldn't it make sense that I'm Linus?"

"Yes, it would make sense, but I've learned in this business never to presume anything without verification. Want to go in the house, show me your driver's license, and answer some questions?"

"I think it doesn't matter what *I* want. It seems to me it only matters what you want."

"You got that right." Maggie nodded at the closest officer. "Randy, can you assist Mr. Anthony to his feet and back into his house?"

"Porch. We sit on the porch. You aren't invited inside my house, and you don't have a warrant so I can keep you out."

The man was right. Maggie nodded. "All right then, we can sit on that stoop at the front of your house that you seem to think qualifies as a porch. Is there even room for any chairs?"

He didn't answer but allowed Randy to help him up and lead him to the front of the house.

There were actually two beat-up old metal chairs under one of the bare dogwood trees. After doing her best to wipe off the old built-up dirt and loose leaves on one chair, Maggie sat. She nodded at the other one. "You can sit there for now. We'll take a look at that license later."

Linus sat. "You think you're going to send someone to get a warrant while you sit out here and talk to me?"

"Nope." She looked down at her fingernails, oddly wondering if it was time to have a manicure. Not that she usually went in for that kind of thing anyway.

"Why not? That seems like some sneaky cop move."

"I'm not trying to be sneaky. All I want is the truth about who you are, where you found the gun, and if you've recently fired a weapon."

"And what if I refuse to give you that information?"

"I can arrest you for obstruction of justice. I won't hesitate to do it, either." Maggie glanced over at Jacob who was in a huddle with the uniformed officers. She wondered what they were discussing. Maybe possible ways to get a warrant. She didn't have time to worry about that. She needed Linus to give something away. Something she could use.

While she focused her attention on her witness, she also kept an eye on her partner. Two of the officers left, and she hoped they were going to radio for a crime scene investigator to come over and do a gunpowder residue test, even though it was probably too late for that to be effective.

Jacob came to stand behind her. The other two officers, including Randy, stayed back a few paces but were close enough to move in if they were needed for any reason.

"Why did you play games today on the phone about the gun? What was the purpose in that if you had no intention of giving us the weapon?"

"Who says I wasn't going to give it to you?"

"When you hung up, wasn't that the clue that you were done with whatever altruistic motive you had when you first called? Makes me wonder, you know."

"Wonder what?"

Maggie scratched her cheek. "If you killed Drusilla and wanted the attention you weren't getting in the media so you came forward as this very helpful friend. It makes sense to me. Happens more than you know."

"What?"

"That someone who acts as if they want to help solve a crime is the one who actually committed it."

Linus laughed. Loudly. "You cannot seriously think I killed Drusilla Isaacs."

"Sure we can. You *said* you have her gun. When we asked you to come in, you hung up the phone. What are we supposed to think when you behave in such a manner?"

"Maybe I was coming around, and maybe I was waiting to hear if the police department was going to move into the twenty-first century and find me by some kind of phone trace." He snickered. "You have to trust me. I would never let anything happen to that gun before I turn it in." He snickered. "I mean nothing worse than has already happened to it—you know, the salt water and the sand."

It finally dawned on Maggie what was going on. She wanted to whack herself in the forehead for her duh moment. "What's it going to take to get you to give it to me? What do you want from the police department?"

Linus clapped his hands together and looked over her shoulder at Jacob. "The lady finally figured it out. Did you?"

"Yeah. You've done something illegal yourself, and you want a deal before you'll cooperate. I get it." Jacob placed a hand on Maggie's shoulder as if he knew she needed it in order to prevent her from coming out of the ratty chair at the man across from her.

"Get me a deal, you get the gun." Linus smirked. "I'll go right in and get it."

The guy just gave them probable cause to search the house, but Maggie played it cool. She'd string him along until the CSIs arrived and then spring it on him.

She reached up and tapped Jacob on the hand that still rested on her shoulder. "Can you go make that phone call we've been waiting to make?"

"Absolutely." Jacob walked away. She could hear him mumbling behind her.

"What call is that he's making?" Linus asked.

"Oh, nothing important. He's checking in with his babysitter to be sure his kid got home from school safely." She shook her head. "I'm always having to remind him to do that." She was lying. Jacob had no children, but this guy didn't know it, and she didn't want to alert him that a warrant would be on the way. He was only cuffed by the hands and could still try to make a break for it if he got suspicious, and she'd prefer not to shoot him if she could help it.

Thinking he was a small time crook, Maggie didn't relish making his life more miserable than it already was, judging by the environment he lived in. Of course, she was giving him the benefit of the doubt on what kind of criminal he was until she could read his rap sheet.

"I'm quite sure you don't expect me to believe that, Detective Blaine. I'd be more inclined to think you were telling me the truth if you said your partner was calling to arrange for the Bolshoi Ballet to come here for a charity performance." Linus leaned forward. "Now, tell me what he's really doing."

She shrugged because by now, they could both see a couple of additional cruisers as well as the crime scene van pulling up at the curb. Linus turned to gape at her before leaping from his chair and knocking it over. He darted away toward the back of the house.

Almost before she could rise, one of the officers who'd been standing by rammed into Linus and slammed him to the ground.

Maggie cringed as they landed. With Linus's hands cuffed, he had no way to soften his fall. His face smacked the grassless ground with a sickening thud.

The man might have been a jerk, but she didn't relish him being hurt in such a manner.

The officer stood and tugged Linus to his feet, keeping hold of his cuffs. Blood poured from Linus's nose.

"Look what you did to me. Police brutality. You broke my nose. All I wanted to do was be a good citizen, and now I have a broken nose."

Jacob stepped over and held a handkerchief out. "If you'll stop yelling, I can help you."

"Why should I stop yelling? I want my neighbors to bear witness to what you've done to me."

"If you want that blood to keep running off your mouth and chin, suit yourself." Jacob shook his head. "I'd think you'd want a bit of assistance."

"Not from anyone with the police department. You need to call an ambulance for me."

"Later. Right now, we have a warrant to serve." Maggie waved the paper in front of Linus's face.

"Warrant? How'd you get that?" Blood flew from his lips as the words spewed from his mouth. "You have no grounds. I want to read it."

Maggie opened the document and held it where Linus could see it.

As he read, he went pale.

Worried about the blood loss from his nose, which seemed to be never ending, Maggie turned to Jacob. "Maybe you should call for some medical assistance."

"No. You're not going to haul me out of here while you ransack my house. I want to be here." Color returned to Linus's face, and a sly grin appeared. "In fact, since you have a warrant to go in to look for the gun, I'll just pop inside and bring it right out to you. No need to mess up my place with all these officers." He nodded at the many law enforcement men and women on his dirt yard.

"You've already shown twice that you're ready to make a run for it, so we'll pass on that invitation," Jacob said. "We'll go in and leave you out here with this officer."

"What if I just tell you where it is? You then can't search anywhere but there, right?"

Knowing Linus was trying to prevent them from finding something else besides the gun, Maggie sprinted toward the house before he could say where the firearm was.

As she reached the door, she heard him yell something, but she couldn't understand it.

Barging into the house, she made her way quickly through the living room which was furnished with a very few pieces. What she would call retro if it was new but would call ratty and old as it were. All of it appeared to have been made in the 1970s. Just a couch, two chairs, a side table, and a lamp. No gun in sight and nowhere to hide one.

She turned the corner to what she presumed would be a bedroom, hearing others entering behind her. Some footsteps headed in the opposite direction. To the kitchen, maybe?

Maggie kept going down a dingy hallway toward the rear of the house. A slightly sour odor reached her, and she gagged.

Placing her hand over her mouth, she kept going, knowing what she smelled now, but hoping it wasn't what she thought it was.

A hand on her shoulder startled her. She jumped. "What?"

"You smell that?" Jacob asked.

"How could I help it?"

"Want me to go first?"

"No. It's fine. Come on." Maggie kept ahead of Jacob, holding her gun out now in case someone was in the bedroom.

She pushed the door open and placed the muzzle of her weapon inside first.

Jacob crept up beside her, and they entered together.

Maggie let out a gasp and stared at the bed.

Jacob found his voice first. "And I thought this guy was just some petty criminal looking for a deal in exchange for a gun."

CHAPTER 7

aggie and Jacob backed out of the room. They stopped at the door back into the living room.

"Everyone out of the house except for the crime scene techs." The other officers left. Maggie addressed the ones who remained. "In the back bedroom is a bad scene. We're going to need you to be extra careful. This guy apparently is a serial killer and has quite a collection of trophies. I suggest those of you with a weak stomach stay out of there since we don't want the scene tainted."

One woman said, "I'm out then. I already have morning sickness, and I sure don't want to be part of that. I'll work out here."

Maggie nodded. "Good plan."

"Do we need to call the coroner?" James, the new guy, asked.

"There's a full body on the bed, but it's partially mummified, so there's no rush on the coroner," Jacob said.

Maggie, still feeling a bit ill herself, said, "Let's leave them to it." She led the way outside and walked straight over to Linus. "You're under arrest. Anything you say can and will be used against you in a court of law—"

Before she could finish, he spat in her face. "Bitch. You should have left me alone. You're next."

Wiping the spittle off her face, hoping for a confession, she said, "Next for what?"

In response, Linus laughed in a bone-chilling way. "Do you really think I'm that stupid?"

Maggie addressed the officer, "Take him to the station and put him in a holding cell. We'll be there when we can break away."

When they were gone, Maggie bent over at the waist and placed her hands on her knees. She took in a number of deep breaths. Finally in a place where she could think straight and process what she'd seen in that bedroom, she stood erect. "What did we just happen upon? I confess, I thought this guy was some kind of attention seeker with a minor record and now this?"

"It was pretty gruesome. I've heard of serial killers keeping souvenirs but actual body parts? Like ears and toes?" Jacob shuddered. "Did I really see nipples? Tell me those were not nipples on that bulletin board."

She shook her head at the memory. "Sorry, I don't think I can."

"What kind of nut job does that and then calls us to taunt us about another crime? It makes no sense. He's obviously gotten away with a lot of murders. Why bring attention to himself now?"

"I'm not a psychologist, but he did seem to be a narcissist—and I only really know about those from my studies and the fact that I believe Drusilla was one—and narcissists like attention. Maybe he wasn't getting any and thought he was too intelligent to get caught. He clearly thought he was smarter than both of us."

"He's been smart for a long time, judging by the number of body parts in that room. It looked like a charnel house." Jacob rubbed his chin. His five o'clock shadow rasped as his palm ran over it. "Do you think he'll plead insanity?"

"I definitely think he's crazy—he'd have to be—but I hope the plea won't fly. He needs to go down and hard."

Jacob sat in the lawn chair vacated by Linus. "Any thoughts about how Linus ties in to Drusilla's murder?"

"I'm thinking he doesn't, but I won't rule anything out yet. It seems weird that he'd show his hand in response to this case. Maybe we need to pay a visit to the department psychologist to see if she can give us any insight."

"Good idea. I'll call her now."

After the coroner left with the mummified body and all the trophies had been bagged and tagged, Maggie and Jacob rode to the station to visit with the psychologist. Letting Linus sit and stew in the holding cell was part of the plan. They usually let a suspect sweat it for a while. Maggie wasn't sure the tactic would work on this one since it was usually more effective on a non-career criminal.

Which reminded her she hadn't seen his rap sheet yet. "Hey, Jacob, call in and see what's what on Linus's sheet."

Jacob called it in and listened on his phone as she drove them toward the station. At one point, he said, "Look up what happened to her, please." When he hung up, he shifted in his seat. "Guess what?"

"What? No record?"

"Not much of one. He had a marijuana charge when he was younger and then nothing until he was stopped for hit and run."

"Anyone hurt?"

"Yeah, but not fatal. The woman he hit was in the hospital for a few weeks with a lot of broken bones. They found his car when he tried to go to a parts yard to get a new fender. I think our boy learned from that how to be sneaky."

"What makes you say that?" She turned into the parking lot.

"It never went to trial."

"Why? Were the charges dismissed?"

"Nope. He got a deal. Probation."

"For a hit and run with injuries? How'd that happen?" Maggie turned the engine off and stared at her partner in amazement.

"The woman moved away and wrote a letter asking that he not be punished too severely."

"That sounds bizarre."

"It is." Jacob shook his head. "And it gets weirder."

"How?"

"The lady ended up as a missing person."

"Say what?" Maggie could scarcely believe it. That was too coincidental. What were the odds that some of those body parts they'd stumbled upon were that woman's?

"Exactly. What do you want to bet that letter was never written by her or was written under duress before he killed her?"

"Geez. This is getting crazier. We have to solve Drusilla's murder and now this? How do we even figure out how to prioritize this stuff?"

"I imagine the captain will have that to deal with. First, those other folks have to be identified, so I say we keep on with the Isaacs's case. At least until Captain Bone says something else."

"But first we talk to the psychologist and then the psycho, okay?" Maggie asked as she opened her car door.

"Sounds like a plan." Jacob winked. "And then some dinner. Once we can get the sights in that bedroom out of our heads."

"Good luck with that."

✃৩✃৩

Ginger McDaniel was waiting in her office when Maggie and Jacob arrived.

She poured them both a cup of coffee. Maggie held hers in both hands, taking some comfort from the heat of the ceramic cup. The things she'd seen in that room were lurking around in her brain, and she wanted to shove them aside and forget them. Maybe the good doctor could help her out on how to make that happen.

Maggie let Jacob take the lead in describing what was in the room as well as the way Linus presented himself in the yard of his home.

Eventually, Maggie said, "He was odd on the phone when I spoke to him earlier in the day. He said he had the gun that belonged to Drusilla, but the crime scene people didn't find it, so I think it's even odder that he would've called to talk about it. I mean, I know there are crackpots out there who like to confess to crimes they didn't commit but this man had so much to lose if any law enforcement came to his house. Why in the world would he ever do such a thing as make a prank call to the police?"

"Lots of reasons exist for why someone does something not in his or her own best interest," Dr. McDaniel said. "But this man sounds like a classic narcissist. I bet if we did an IQ exam, we'd find he's highly intelligent."

"Yes, he definitely seemed so but why do something so stupid?" Maggie asked.

"Because of the narcissism. He thought he would outsmart you. That you'd never even find him."

"He did say something about us not being able to trace him. We got lucky, and there was a young lady who overheard the conversation at a pay phone. She called in the tag number," Jacob said.

"That seems unusual, too." Dr. McDaniel made a steeple with her fingers and rested her chin on the tip for a moment. "I have to wonder if that young lady was in on it. If she and this Linus know each other and he got her to give you the information."

"But that makes no sense. We'd for sure catch him then." Maggie shook her head. "The girl wasn't involved."

"Have you checked her out?" the doctor asked.

"No, but we will." Jacob placed a hand on Maggie's forearm where it rested on the chair across from the doctor's desk. "It can't hurt to see what her record is, can it?"

"No, but if he thought we wouldn't find him with a trace of the phone call, why would he then give out his tag number like that?" Maggie was totally confused. None of it made sense.

"Again, I go back to him wanting to prove he could outsmart the police. He must have truly believed he could. It was a game to him. Taunt you with it. You fail to get what you want, and he wins." Dr. McDaniel leaned forward. "How did he act when you showed up at his door?"

"Smug. Like we'd never get a warrant," Jacob said.

"And we wouldn't have until he slipped and said 'give me a deal and you get the gun.' That told us he'd committed a crime and gave us probable cause to search his home. Especially when he added he could go right in and get it for us." Maggie smiled at the doctor. "That's where he messed up, and he didn't even realize it."

"And when the warrant got there, what did he do?"

Jacob laughed. "First, he tried to run and then when he was caught, he made a big deal of accusing us of breaking his nose." He rubbed his own nose. "And that makes me wonder if he was trying to create a diversion to make us give up the search and take him to a hospital."

"Probably. I'd bet on it. He thought you'd never get the warrant and he was safe to taunt you." Doctor McDaniel stood. "If he raises insanity as a plea, I imagine I'll get a chance to chat with him and could give you more information then." She smiled. "For now, though, I have a dinner date so I'll have to wait to find out how your interrogation goes."

Jacob stood as well. "Dinner sounds great. I think I'll try to talk my partner into doing the same thing so we can go into interrogation at least with full stomachs if not with a night's sleep."

"You don't have to ask me twice. Let's go." Maggie rose and practically jogged out of the station. Suddenly, she was starving, and it seemed like days since she last ate.

They walked down the street to Full Moon BBQ. They both loved the baby back ribs, and since it was so close to the police department, the waitresses knew them by name.

Their normal drink orders almost made it to their table before they did.

Taking a seat, Jacob glanced up at the waitress. Before he could say anything, she said, "Baby back ribs and corn for both of you, right?"

"One day we're going to order something different and shock you," Maggie said.

"Warn me ahead of time so I can make sure I have my nitroglycerin on hand to stop the heart attack." The waitress walked away, laughing at her own joke.

"What do you think about questioning Linus?" Jacob smiled over the top of his glass of tea. "He seemed to take a liking to the way you bantered with him so I think I should be the bad cop."

Maggie frowned. "You know I like to be the bad cop."

"I think it's too late with this guy. He's already been overexposed to you. First on the phone and then at his house. It's going to be better for me to be the jerk since he doesn't have as clear a picture of me as he does you."

"I know you're right. I'll adapt."

Their food came, and they ate quickly, knowing they needed to get back to the station to at least start the interrogation of the serial killer. Maggie was sure at some point there would be additional detectives chatting with the man. They'd need lots of help in getting identifications on the large number of victims she presumed there were, based on the items in that bedroom.

Locating the rest of the bodies and giving the families closure on their missing loved ones would be a lot of work as well. How they'd stumbled on this mess was still befuddling to her.

It made no sense, and she worried that thought in her mind while she ate the ribs.

The waitress brought the bill. Angela from the crime scene division followed behind her.

Jacob had his wallet in his hand. He stopped pulling his debit card out as Angela sat beside Maggie and across from him. "What's going on, Angela? We're already done eating. We can't stay and keep you company."

"I'm not here to eat," Angela said with a look on her face that Maggie couldn't read.

"What is it?" Maggie asked. "What's happened?"

"When we left Linus Anthony's house, we had his car towed to the impound yard and just completed a search of it."

"Did you find Drusilla's gun?" Maggie thought that would be a good thing, but it didn't explain the strange way Angela was staring at Jacob.

Angela tore her eyes from Jacob's and said, "Yes. It's being tested now. It was in the trunk." She turned to Jacob. "There were some other things in the wheel-well of the trunk."

Jacob's face went pale. "Things like what?"

Suddenly fearful of what Angela was going to disclose, Maggie's heart sank. Her hand moved of its own volition and knocked her plastic glass to the floor. It bounced along with what sounded like three quick shots in succession.

Placing an evidence bag on the table, Angela slid it across toward Jacob. "I worked in the lab when your wife was killed. As I recall, when she was found in your kitchen, she was missing some pieces of jewelry that she always wore."

He nodded but didn't touch the bag. If anything, he was even more ashen.

"I'm sorry, Jacob. I didn't want to show you this at the station as I wanted you to have a chance to recover before you went back. I think these are your wife's. The one earring matches the one you carry with you." She held her hand up. "No need to deny it. We've all seen you take it out of your pocket and fiddle with it."

Jacob stared at the bag but still didn't make a move. "Okay. So what? There's an earring that matches. It doesn't mean anything. It's not like Debra had a one of a kind piece."

"There's also the charm bracelet with your wedding date on the bride and groom charm and that one you showed me you got her for her last birthday. You know, the one with the silver sneaker and the date of her first marathon you had engraved on it." Angela reached over and touched Jacob's hand. "I'm very sorry to have to tell you all this."

Jacob shook his head in denial. "My wife was a victim of Linus Anthony? How can that be? Debra was left whole, complete. There were no missing parts. We've seen he takes trophies."

This was good news and bad news. Jacob's wife had been stabbed in their kitchen, and the case was unsolved. Now they had a suspect, but Jacob was in denial.

"Will you take a look in the bag?" Maggie asked him.

"Outside. Not in here." He stood abruptly and shoved his chair back. He strode out of the restaurant, followed by Angela with the plastic baggie.

Maggie pulled some money from her wallet and laid it on the table, paying for both their meals and the tip.

She passed a few officers she recognized on her way out. Many looked at her with puzzled expressions.

Outside, she didn't see Angela or Jacob.

Unsure where they were, she headed toward the station, intent on talking to Captain Bone about removing

Jacob from the interrogation of Linus. He couldn't very well go in there, now that they had proof that the man was a suspect in the murder of Jacob's wife.

As to the lack of a trophy from Debra, perhaps when Linus killed her, it was one of his earliest murders. Maybe the taking of jewelry from the deceased had escalated into taking body parts as he became more practiced in the act of murder. After all, Debra had been dead almost two years now.

Then it hit Maggie. If Debra was one of his first murders, Linus had been very busy for the past two years. There hadn't been that many missing people in town in that time. He must have hunted farther afield.

Shaking her head at all the odd turns this case was taking, Maggie focused on getting to the station ahead of Jacob.

Turning the corner, she stopped in her tracks.

CHAPTER 8

Jacob crouched against the brick exterior of the building as if he'd slid down the wall where he stood. In his hand, Maggie could see the baggie. He seemed to be staring at it in a daze. Angela stood beside him as if at a loss about what to do.

Maggie strode forward. She held her hand out to her partner. "Come on. Let's get you up. We need to talk to the captain. Another team needs to take on Linus's interrogation."

He ignored her hand. "No. We're going to take this bastard down. He killed Debra, and he's mine."

"You know it doesn't work that way. You need to come to terms with that. So come on. Let's get to the station and chat with Captain Bone. We're going to stay on

Drusilla's case but let someone else take on Linus. If we're going to get a conviction, that's what we have to do." Maggie shook her still proffered hand. "Now."

This time Jacob took it and let her tug him to his feet. "But I don't have to like it."

"That's the truth. I hate it too, but there's not a damn thing we can do about it."

He seemed a bit better and not so out of it, but Maggie noticed he still had a death grip on the baggie.

Angela led the way, and they were soon at the door to the stationhouse. Jacob reluctantly let go of the baggie so Angela could return it to the lab and then the evidence room.

As Maggie and Jacob walked toward the captain's office, Maggie said, "Don't tell Captain Bone Angela took that jewelry out of the station. That could get her in a lot of trouble. She took a risk bringing to us."

"I won't say anything. At least she didn't break the chain of custody since she said she took it from the trunk herself."

"That's good." Maggie rapped on the glass on the upper part of the door.

Captain Bone waved them in. "Glad to see you two back from dinner. I want you to go home now and get some rest before picking up on the Isaacs murder tomorrow. I have to take you off Linus Anthony since we now suspect him of being complicit in Debra's murder."

"I know. Angela told us." Jacob's eyes filled with unshed tears. "It's good that we have a lead now in catching her murderer, but I feel like someone placed duct tape on my eyebrows and ripped it off all at once, making me lose all my brow-hair. It hurts like an open, festering sore now." He ran a hand over his face. "Like it's fresh and new all over again."

"All the more reason to go home then. Take one of those nighttime sleep aids and rest," the captain said.

Jacob nodded. "I will. Sounds like a good way to try to forget…at least for tonight."

"You go on, too, Maggie. Tomorrow is soon enough. We'll handle the interrogation of Anthony tonight."

"Be sure you have whoever is doing it keep him up all night with no food and little to drink." Maggie knew they'd have to feed the man something, but they would hold off for a while. It was a basic interrogation tactic. Get them tired, hungry, and thirsty and then have the person playing good cop offer to get some things to make the prisoner comfortable. It helped build trust.

"He'll get dinner, Detective." Captain Bone looked at her watch. "In about three hours."

"Who's in there with him?" Maggie asked.

"Jeffery Stutsman and Joy Winslow."

"Super. They'll do great. Jeff is an old pro, and Joy is coming along nicely in her interrogation skills. I sat in on one with her last week." Maggie smiled at the memory of just how great Joy was at playing bad cop. She'd nailed that guy in her interrogation. Maggie also knew Jeff would be perfect for whatever game of cat and mouse Linus Anthony might try to play. Jeff was brilliant and would hold his own with that nut job.

"Make sure your partner gets home safely before you head home yourself," Captain Bone said.

Maggie nodded before following her partner down the hall. She didn't need to tell the captain that her partner wouldn't be returning to his own house that evening. He was staying at her place as long as he needed to.

Out in the parking lot, Jacob stood at Maggie's car. "Can we go by my place for a minute?"

"Are you sure?"

"Positive." He opened his door when she clicked the unlock button on her keychain.

Inside the car, as she backed out of the parking space, Maggie cast a look in her partner's direction. He seemed all right at the moment, but she was worried about why he wanted to swing by his house.

He sat silently in the passenger seat all the way. When they turned into his neighborhood, he said, "Come inside with me?"

"Of course."

They went in the front door. Maggie followed Jacob through the foyer and around the corner to the kitchen. He stopped so fast, she almost plowed into his back.

Pointing across the room toward the refrigerator, he said, "There. Over there was where I found her. I came in from work by the front door. She always used the garage for her car, and I parked down the driveway. Sometimes, she'd leave the garage door open, and I could come that way, but that day, it was down." Jacob turned to Maggie with a blank look in his eyes. "My whole life was about to change, and I was a little peeved because she closed that door and I had two bags of items I'd picked up at the store for her. She hadn't left the door up, and I was muttering about it when I came around this corner and saw her there, covered in blood." He shuddered and almost went down to the floor. Maggie grabbed his arm and held him up. In a few moments, he said, "How can I ever forgive myself for not being here to help her and worse, for mulling over in my mind what I was going to say to her about closing the garage door and forcing me to juggle my keys to unlock that front door?"

Maggie didn't let go of Jacob. "Have you been carrying that load all this time?"

"Yes. There I was thinking of fighting with my wife, and she'd already fought for her life and lost it. I felt like a jerk of the first degree."

"There was no way you could know any of that. You have to stop beating yourself up over it. We both know you loved Debra and would never have wanted her hurt. She also knew you loved her, and I'm quite sure her last thoughts were of you."

"Yeah." He let out a bark of a laugh. "Like wondering why the hell I wasn't here to save her."

Maggie let go of Jacob and walked across the hardwood floor. "Where does this door lead?"

"That's the pantry."

She pointed to another door a few feet farther away. "What's that one over there?"

"The door to the garage."

"That the one you'd come in if she'd left the outer door to the garage open?"

"Yeah. Why?"

She stepped over and opened it. Feeling along the drywall, she found the switch for the garage door and pressed it. The door slid open easily. Maggie hesitated to say what she wanted to say to say but, eventually, she decided it couldn't make him feel any worse, and it might help him.

Taking a deep breath, she said, "Consider this."

"What?" Jacob walked toward her. "The door's open?"

"Right." She nodded. "What if it was open, that day and Linus saw that?"

"God, that would be even worse, Mags. Then it would mean her being nice enough to leave it up for me led directly to her death as it gave him the way inside."

"But remember, the investigation found the point of entry was the window in the bedroom you said she always left open and you nagged her to close it?"

Jacob ran his hand over his eyes. "Yeah, so now you're saying he may have come in this way."

"No. What I'm saying is that Linus shut that door just like I opened it. From inside this room. He probably figured there'd be less chance of someone coming in while he was here or soon after he left if the door was down."

"You really think that could have been what happened?"

"Makes sense to me. He was in here stealing her jewelry and killing her. He wanted not to be rushed. He came in the back window so he clearly didn't know the garage was open as that would've been a super easy entry."

Jacob paced the space for a few minutes. Maggie stood where she was, giving him time to process what she'd said.

Finally, he stopped in exactly the place where he'd found his wife's body. He knelt and put his palm on the floor. "I'm so sorry, Debra. I've not been able to forgive myself for not saving you. Now that we've caught the man responsible, I have to try to blame him and not me. Please." He stood. "I'm ready to go, but I see myself returning home soon. Once we get this guy indicted, I think I'll be able to sleep in my own bed again."

"I'm glad. Not that I mind you staying at my place."

"I know. You're the best, but I do see I need to make my way back here."

Maggie walked to the front door. Over her shoulder, she said, "You actually don't. You could always sell and then start over in a new house. There are no rules about what you have to do as an adult."

"Even though only you and I know I've been sleeping at your house since two weeks after Debra died, I still need to man up and quit leaning on you," Jacob said as he locked the front door.

When they arrived at Maggie's house, they sat in front of the television for a while watching an old movie. Maggie knew Jacob wasn't paying the least attention to it, but she somehow thought he wasn't ready to go into his room and be alone, so she sat with him.

Casting a glance in his direction periodically, she was positive he wasn't even aware of where he was. He seemed far away and deep in thought.

Eventually, he said, "I know you're only out here to be sure I'm okay. Go on to bed. I'm going to do the same."

Maggie faced him and searched his eyes to try to see how he really was. "Are you sure?"

Jacob stood and left her sitting on the couch. "Positive."

Shrugging her shoulders, she stopped in the kitchen for a glass of ice water and then went to bed.

After what seemed like an hour but was closer to three when Maggie looked at the clock on her nightstand, she felt someone sit on the bed.

Rolling over, she glanced up to see her partner, pale and wide-eyed.

She sat up. "What is it?"

"Sorry. I've been trying to deal, but every time I close my eyes, I see Linus Anthony killing Debra. I've always said if I could just know who did it, I could have closure, but I was wrong. Now that I know who did it, it's worse as I see the face of her murderer."

Maggie reached out for him. "Come here. You can lay with me. There's no need in being awake alone."

"I didn't want to bother you, but I couldn't think of anything else to do besides pace your living room."

"It's not a bother. At least try to rest, even if you can't sleep."

He reclined on the extra pillows on the other side of the bed. "Don't tell anyone we slept together." He tried to laugh but it came out more like a strangled sound.

"But you said you aren't going to sleep, so I can't say that anyway."

"Ha. That's even worse. Spending time in bed without sleeping will be the talk of the precinct."

"I'm taking a vow of silence." Maggie reached to the foot of the bed and pulled a quilt toward him. "If you're going to be here, you may as well have some covers."

"Thanks, Mags. You really are the best." He settled in, and she turned over on her side, unsure if he would sleep but knowing she needed to in order to be ready to get back on the trail of Drusilla's murderer in a few hours when their shift started.

When the rising sun peeked through the slit in the curtains, Maggie woke and realized Jacob had been able to fall asleep after all. He was breathing deeply and had snuggled his body up to hers.

Unsure what to do as she didn't want to disturb him, she stayed as she was for a few minutes.

Eventually, he stretched and seemed to realize where he was. He practically leapt off the bed, taking the quilt with him and landing in a tangle on the floor.

ℂℂℂ

After quick showers and an awkward moment at breakfast before they laughed it off, Maggie and Jacob headed to the station in his car.

Captain Bone met them in the bullpen. "You have company in interview one."

"We don't even get to hear what happened with Linus Anthony?" Jacob asked.

"Or get coffee?" Maggie asked.

"Don't try to fool me, Detective Blaine. I'm quite sure you've already main-lined two cups.

Maggie shrugged and laughed. "Thought I'd try."

The captain turned to Jacob. "We'll brief you later. Stutsman and Winslow did a great job, but right now, you need to tend to the woman in interview one." Captain Bone walked toward her office.

Knowing she meant her words as an order, even though they were uttered mildly, Maggie and Jacob headed to the interview room.

They stepped over the threshold to find Anne Leighton in a state of agitation, pacing the area behind the table. Oddly, she'd cut her hair off since the day before.

"Good morning, Ms. Leighton. How can we be of assistance today?" Jacob sat on the edge of the table and swung one leg casually. It only emphasized the furor of Anne's movements.

She raked her hands thorough short, spiky hair, making it stick out even more. "I've got to get back into Drusilla's office today. The crime scene tape is still up, and I don't want to get in trouble for going in."

"Have you been over there?" Maggie asked.

"Yes, I went at six this morning, and that crazy old woman across the street started yelling at me when I put my key in the lock. She said you were her friend and she was going to call you if I didn't leave and put that tape back." Anne leaned her knuckles on the table and glared at Maggie. "You have no right to have that old bat spy for you. No right at all."

"First of all, did you actually remove the yellow tape from the door?" Jacob asked.

"I moved it aside in order to put my key in the lock, but before I could do anything else, that woman screeched at me from her front porch."

Maggie wanted to cheer for Hattie Simpkins being on the ball this morning. She was definitely going to go by and check on the woman. Her actions stopped whatever Anne had planned to do.

Jacob looked over to where Maggie stood with her back against the door. "How weird is it that Drusilla Isaacs hired a woman to be her assistant who can't even read?"

Maggie scratched her head as if confused. "It does seem strange, doesn't it?"

"You two think you're funny, but you're not. I *need* to get into that office, and I want you to make it happen." Anne stormed over to where Jacob sat and stopped right in front of him. "Now."

"I'm sorry, Miss Leighton, you're somehow mistaken about what kind of demands you can make here. You seem to be forgetting a lady was killed, and we're trying to bring her murderer to justice. We can't let anyone in that building until it's cleared by the crime scene techs. Whatever you need is going to have to wait." Jacob got off the table.

"I refuse to agree to that. We need to get in there."

"We?" Maggie asked.

"Me. I meant *me*."

Wondering who Anne really meant by *we* since she slipped and used the word, Maggie asked, "What do you need? Perhaps we can get one of the crime scene officers to get your item for you."

"No. That won't work. That's not going to be acceptable." Anne paced again for a few moments. Suddenly, she stopped and whirled around to face Maggie. Opening her purse, Anne pulled out her wallet.

Jacob shook his head. "You don't want to do that, Miss Leighton."

"Shut up." Anne took a handful of cash from the wallet. "This is about three-hundred dollars. Will that get me in there for about ten minutes?"

"Absolutely not," Maggie said. She turned to her partner. "Jacob, tell the lady what she just bought."

Jacob held out his cuffs. "You're under arrest for attempting to bribe a law enforcement officer, you have the right to remain silent—"

Anne collapsed to the floor and let out a wail. "You can't do this. I've done nothing wrong. All I want to do is go inside and get something. It can't be illegal." She sat and sobbed.

Jacob nodded at Maggie. "Please assist Miss Leighton to her feet so I can cuff her and take her to booking."

When they had her up, Maggie said, "I'll leave you to process her, and I'll be going to take care of what we need to do from here."

Maggie was sure Jacob knew she meant she was going back to the crime scene to see what exactly they had missed that was so urgent to be removed from the premises. No way would Anne Leighton be so spun up unless there was something incriminating in that building.

He nodded and tossed her his car keys. "Take mine."

Keeping herself from laughing since her own car was at her house, Maggie took the keys and left.

On her way out, she stopped by the lab and asked James Windsor to accompany her so he could bag and tag whatever they might find.

CHAPTER 9

When they pulled into the parking lot at Drusilla's building, Hattie Simpkins came out her front door and called out, "Mornin' Detective. I'm glad to see you. That secretary of Miz Isaacs was here trying to break in. I shooed her away, but I've been watching to see if she was gonna come back."

"Thanks, Mrs. Simpkins. I'm glad you were watching out. I've got to go in for a minute or two, but I'll come to see you and my friend, Mordecai, before I go back to the station."

"I'll be here. Bring that handsome fella with you. We'll have a piece of cake."

"I will." Maggie smiled at James. "I hope you like food. That woman is all about feeding people."

"Sounds like she really likes you." He opened the door after unlocking it.

"She seems lonely, and since she's so kind, I feel like I should try to be nice in return."

"Nothing wrong with that."

They went inside, and Maggie headed directly to Anne's desk. She pulled some latex gloves out of her pocket and opened the top drawer.

"What are we looking for?" James asked.

"Not sure. All I know is the victim's secretary was at the station today desperate to get in here and get something. I'm curious about what she could want." Maggie rifled through the drawers but didn't see anything suspicious.

James was going through a cabinet. "Do you think she participated in the murder?"

"I have no idea yet. I've not really made any suppositions thus far. To tell the truth, this one is a convoluted mess. I mean, how often do you see someone attacked in so many ways, all at once?"

"Are you leaning toward some kind of conspiracy? I mean, really, how could that have all happened on the same day? I think someone could decide to poison a person, easy. And I think some guy could decide to shoot another one, but for those to be done at the same moment seems a stretch, doesn't it?"

"Exactly." Maggie moved on to look inside the credenza where a number of photos and a laser printer sat. "I think it had to be something along the lines of an attempt to poison her and when she didn't succumb, someone stabbed her. She got away and outside the building. At that point, it became a crime of opportunity. Some unknown person who had a grudge against her saw their chance to shoot her, and when she still didn't go down, she was strangled."

"And no one saw anything? What about the gun? Angela said that came into the lab yesterday, but I haven't heard about any results yet, have you—well, hello."

"What?" Maggie glanced up, thinking he was greeting someone coming in but he was holding up a small vial with some white powder in it.

She stepped over to him and peered at it. "What do you think it is?"

"Not sure but since it was hidden behind six reams of paper and inside an empty box of staples. I think it's going back to the lab with me for some tests." He pulled out a baggie, put the vial and staple box inside, dated, and initialed it.

"Could that be our poison?"

"Maybe. Or it could be cocaine. I don't want to open it here, but it looks like the same consistency."

"I don't see either of them as cokeheads, but I guess you never really know."

"Until I get it to the lab." James laughed. "Let's see what else we can find." He moved to the bathroom. Maggie could hear him plundering around in there.

"I think that room was checked pretty thoroughly," she called out.

"Now that I've found that little gem hidden away, I'm on a quest to see what else that woman may have cleverly disguised."

Maggie shrugged. Let the new guy recheck the area all he wanted. Who knew, he might get lucky again.

She went into Drusilla's office and stood by the door, looking over the whole room, trying to recreate what might have happened.

Picturing Drusilla having her coffee while checking email or sifting through phone messages led Maggie to wonder if Drusilla felt the effects of the poison in her drink and staggered to her feet.

Then had whoever was here with her decided the poison wasn't working fast enough and used the knife on her for good measure? But then how had they let her get out of the office and on to the street?

Walking around the room, Maggie pretended to be Drusilla. They knew she'd put her bloody hand on the edge of the desk and then the wall. Where would her attacker be while this was happening? Why leave her alive?

Did the phone ring? Or did someone come by and need to be deflected?

"Hey, James, have you found anything else?" she called into the other room.

"Nope." He poked his head inside. "Not yet. Why?"

"Just wondered. I'm going to call Jacob and get him to pull the phone records to see if any calls came in here after the likely time of the stabbing. I was thinking there had to be some kind of diversion—either a call or someone popping in without an appointment—for the first person or persons who were trying to kill her to leave her alone long enough to allow her to somehow get outside."

James quirked his eyebrows. "How about this? Our secretary with the vial of white powder has a boyfriend who came by and either kissed her into oblivion or even better, had sex with her on the floor here or the conference room desk."

Maggie tilted her head and opened her eyes wide. "Did we test for semen on those surfaces?"

"Yeah, right. That's a standard thing to do in murders in an office setting."

"If you're right, sounds like something that needs to be put in the manual. Do you have the equipment or do you need to call for a van?"

"I'm calling now." He pulled out his phone and scrolled down to the contact number. "You may as well go visit your little lady while I'm doing this. Be sure to get her to wrap me a piece of cake, okay?"

"Sure. I think she wanted to flirt with the handsome CSI, but she'll have to be happy with me." Maggie grinned. "Let me know if you come up with any other theories. You're pretty good at that."

She walked out to the sound of his laughter and

strolled across the street toward Hattie's house. Before she got to the porch, the woman was on it with her gray cat in her arms. "Where's your man friend?"

"He's a coworker and is tied up right now. He said to tell you to save him some cake."

"Tied up? Lord, girl, you got that cute boy tied up, and you ain't over there making a move on him? What's wrong with your generation?"

Maggie reached out and ran a hand over Mordecai's back. "You sure you aren't a comedian at one of the clubs? You're making me laugh."

"You gotta admit, he *is* a nice looking young man."

"He is at that, Miss Hattie. I'm just not looking for that kind of thing right now."

"Nonsense. But if you're determined not to find a man, come on in and let me fatten you up with some good food." Hattie opened her screen door and led the way in.

Maggie followed her in and to the kitchen where she sat at the table.

While Hattie pulled out a couple of plates, Maggie said, "How about getting down one more?"

"You think your boy will be coming after all?"

"No, but I have a friend who lives in the apartments over across the street, and he sure could use a piece of cake. Mind if I invite him?"

"Of course not. If you've got a man you want to entertain, I'm glad to help you."

Maggie didn't tell her she was really calling the veteran, John Hays, because she thought they would be good for each other.

The veteran arrived almost as soon as Maggie disconnected the call.

He knocked on the screen door and called out as he entered, "It's me. Hays."

Maggie was surprised at how fast the man could move to get out of his apartment and across the street, especially when he was so slow getting out of his chair the day before.

"Turn to the right. We're in the kitchen," Hattie said in a voice that carried across the house. She lowered it to say to Maggie, "I like a man who's not one to stand on ceremony and wait for my old bones to hobble to the front door."

"There you go again making me laugh. You move better than some women I've seen who are half your age." Maggie smiled at John as he came into view. "Mr. Hays, this is my friend, Hattie Simpkins."

"Nice to meet you, Ms. Simpkins." His eyes settled on the cake. "Hey, is that coconut? My grandmother always kept one on her dining room table."

"Mine, too, Mr. Hays. Mine, too. I use her recipe."

"Mine cracked her own coconuts and used the meat as well as the milk."

"So did mine." Hattie winked. "And so do I. Come on and dig in and tell me who's is better."

"Oh, I'll dig in for sure. I haven't had good coconut cake like hers since I got back from 'Nam." He grinned. "But even if yours is better, I can't say since my Grandma Rose would never forgive me—even from beyond the grave."

"We can't have that, so sit on down and lie to me that your gran's was better than mine." Hattie cut John a huge slice as he pulled out a chair.

No one spoke as they all dug into the sweetness of the cake.

In a few moments, John looked up with bliss reflected on his face. "That was good enough for all the saints in heaven to want a slice."

"Even your grandmother?" Maggie asked.

Hattie chuckled. "I'm going to take that as an admission about the quality of my cooking."

"You sure can, Ms. Simpkins."

"Come now, you have to call me Hattie now that I've fed you what you think is the nectar of the gods." Hattie poured them each a glass of tea from the pitcher on the table.

"I'll call you Angel instead because surely you're an angel on Earth." He grinned. "And I'm John."

"You mean you're the devil with your pretty blue eyes and your compliments to turn an old woman's head."

Maggie was thrilled they were hitting it off. She glanced down at her watch. "I better get back to it. I'm sure my crime scene tech is done by now."

"Before you go, can you tell us anything about the case? Should we be worried there's an insane killer on the loose?" John asked.

Happy she could tell them at least one lunatic was off the street, Maggie said, "We think Drusilla was killed by someone who knew her well so you're most likely safe. We don't know who yet but in the process of our investigation, we seem to have stumbled upon a serial killer who we were able to arrest so that's good news, right?"

Hattie put her hand to her breast. "Lord, child, that's scary."

John leaned over and touched Hattie's hand. "Let me give you my phone number. If you get scared, you can call me any time. I'm just across the road."

"At least he's in custody now." Maggie stood and left them there chatting. As she opened the screen door to head back across the street, Mordecai meowed at her. "I know. He's a stranger, but I think it'll be fine. You'll learn to like him."

Feeling a little foolish for chatting with a cat, Maggie glanced around to be sure she wasn't heard.

On the porch stood James. "I had no idea you spoke cat." He laughed then looked down at her empty hands. "I was under the impression you were bringing me some cake. Did you eat it all?"

Before she could answer, Hattie came out with a foil

wrapped package. "You forgot this for your handsome friend."

"I was just asking about that." James took the proffered cake. "And thanks for the handsome. I haven't had a compliment from such a beautiful lady in many years."

"You really are a terrible liar." Hattie poked him in the chest. "I bet all the girls like you."

"Speaking of handsome men, shouldn't you get back to John?" Maggie asked. They really needed to go but she didn't want to be rude to her new friend.

"All right. I understand." Hattie grinned. "You need to be on your way."

Maggie smiled and nodded. She stepped off the porch, pulled the keys out of her pocket and walked toward the street. "I'll see you later." Whispering to James, Maggie asked, "Did you find anything else?" She handed him the keys. "You can drive us back."

"I found another vial. This one was hidden in a partially emptied tampon box." He winked. "The extra absorbent kind."

"And that part is important?"

"Nope. Just wanted to say it."

"Ha, ha. Can you tell what's in the vial by looking?"

"If my knowledge of the Physician's Desk Reference isn't too rusty, I believe it's Lortab. I'll have to test it, of course."

"Was it full?"

"Nope. There are six whole tablets and one that was

cut in half. There's also some residue on the bottom." He opened his car door.

"Could they be the poison Doc Martinez says she ingested? Like crushed into a drink or something?"

"Too many can kill, but it wouldn't show as a poison in a tox screen. Once we know what's in the two vials, we'll have Doc check for those substances." He grimaced. "Unless the body has been released and cremated."

"I don't think it has, but now that you mention it, I did hear Drusilla's husband was asking when he could arrange to have her taken to the funeral home. It always makes me nervous when they're anxious for that."

"You're such a cynic."

"Years of being a homicide detective will do that to even the sweetest former homecoming queen." She settled into the passenger seat.

"You were homecoming queen?" He looked her over. "Yeah, I can see that."

"I didn't say I *was*. I was just making an observation."

"Oh, so you're one of those women. I guess it's good to learn that early in my career here."

"What women?"

"The ones that I like—you know, not afraid to give a man some grief—of course, I mean that only in the kindest way possible."

"In the man's world I work in, it's something I don't

even think about anymore." Maggie held up her hand. "Before you say anything about that, yes, it *is* still a man's world, even though there are a lot more females in law enforcement now."

He nodded and drove on.

When they got back to the station, James parked the car and grabbed the two bagged vials he had on the seat beside them. "I'll rush these and let you know what I find. I'll call Doc Martinez, too."

"Thanks. I'll be around."

Maggie strolled down the hallway trying to find Jacob. She wondered if he got anything useful out of Anne Leighton. And now she couldn't wait to see what James learned about the substances in the vials so she could interrogate her about them and who would've hidden them in the office.

She stopped for some coffee and ran into Jacob plundering through the cabinets.

"What are you doing?"

"Oh, hey. Did you find anything?" he asked.

"Yeah. A couple of vials of stuff—maybe Lortab in one and who knows in the other."

"I'm starving. You got any crackers or anything?"

"In my desk. What did you learn from our friend?"

"Nothing much. How did the crime scene techs miss the vials?" Jacob led the way to the bullpen. "Come on and share some crackers with me."

"You're always hungry."

"Interrogation makes me want to eat."

"Eat food or eat someone alive?" She laughed, opened the large bottom drawer of her desk and tossed him a sleeve of Ritz crackers.

"Both." Jacob flopped into his chair and leaned his elbows on the top of his own desk, shoving a file aside and digging into the snack.

"But Anne didn't come off with much?" Maggie asked.

"Nope. She just kept saying she wanted back in the office because there were some clients who were calling and demanding their records so they could go to other accountants. All she wanted was to get those people off her back."

"Yeah, not buying that. Those two vials were hidden pretty well. One in a box of staples and one in a half-full box of tampons, so someone either had a drug problem or was using those substances for a murder weapon."

"Looks like our girl will be staying in a bit longer. They've set her bond hearing for tomorrow. I should call the state's attorney and let them know about the new discoveries. They may want to ask for a higher bond since that's a bit more serious than trying to break the crime scene tape to gain access." He grinned. "But I'll call after I finish these." He waggled the cracker sleeve back and forth.

The phone on Maggie's phone rang. "Blaine."

She listened for a few moments then replaced the receiver. Looking at her partner, she said, "Better take those to go. We've got a break in at Drusilla's house, and, according to the caller, the guy is still inside."

CHAPTER 10

Arriving at Drusilla's house, Jacob and Maggie parked two driveways away and waited for the uniform officers to clear the house. The first ones on the scene had captured one man as he exited. He'd indicated he was alone, but proper procedure was to be sure the house was empty by sending in dogs and officers.

Maggie and Jacob stepped onto the porch where the officers stood with their prisoner.

"How are you doing this pretty, sunny day, David Isaacs?" Maggie asked.

"Why are you trying to arrest me for being in my own house?" He glared at her in indignation as if he were in the right for being there.

"This isn't your property. It's your former wife's, and she's dead. What would you be needing in there?" Jacob asked.

"How do you know it's not mine? I was on the deed."

"*Was* being the operative word, right? When you got divorced, you stayed on there for a while until Drusilla paid you off, and you signed it over to her, right?" Maggie remembered that much from when she and the victim had been friendly. Drusilla whined a lot about him refusing to come and sign the deed so she could refinance. Maggie had never heard if he'd actually signed the thing. She'd have to check with the deed registry.

"Why does it matter? I used to live here. I remembered something I forgot to take when I moved out. Figured I'd come get it while I could. Before the probate process started and there was confusion about ownership."

Maggie looked at the officer standing beside the cuffed prisoner. "What did he have on him when you got him?"

"These." The officer held out a purple Crown Royal bag. It made a jangling noise as he passed it along to her."

Peering inside, Maggie let out a small gasp. She turned to Jacob. "Hold your hands out."

Jacob cupped his hands, and she turned the bag over. A pile of gold coins landed in them. "Well, there you go,

Isaacs. I would bet these belonged to your former wife."

"Why? You can't prove that, and I knew exactly where they were since they're mine."

Jacob poured the coins back in the bag Maggie held open. "She was an accountant and savvy about investments. You work at a gym, and even though there's nothing wrong with that, Drusilla had more income than you and would be more likely to invest in gold."

"That's a lot of stereotyping, and I resent it. Just give me my coins, and I won't sue you for false arrest."

"Dude, you are on your way to lock up so you may as well give up that line of bull." Jacob nodded at the uniformed officer. "Haul him in. We'll follow in a while."

Once David was gone and the house completely clear, Maggie and Jacob went inside to look around.

The place was neat but cluttered just as it had been when they questioned Curtis. The man had clearly made no effort to neaten it. It must have been the way they lived all the time.

Weirdly, when they'd been so-called friends, Drusilla never invited her inside if Maggie came by to pick her up to drive her somewhere or even just to leave her car there while Drusilla drove. Now she thought she might know why she'd never been let in.

Now that they had a chance to look around without the man of the house present, they turned on more lights than Curtis had on when they'd been there before. The furniture was shabbier than Maggie remembered from the first visit. It also appeared the woman had a hoarding problem when it came to *TV Guide* and *Cosmopolitan Magazines*. They were on every surface and even stacked beside two chairs.

"Good grief, do you think she ever threw away a magazine?" Jacob asked.

"Don't think so. Kind of odd. I'd never have guessed it." Maggie moved out of the living room and down the hall to what looked to be several bedrooms and a home office. "Nothing looks disturbed so maybe the only thing he wanted was those coins."

"Yeah, but you know, let's check out her room. My mother always said to keep the valuable stuff you don't want to lose in your underwear drawer. Maybe her mom did, too." Jacob went into the master bedroom and straight to the dresser, Maggie right behind him.

"Don't you know all criminals know that rule? I bet she heard it and ignored it."

Jacob held up two small jewelry boxes. "Look here what I found in among the undies."

"See what's in there. I bet it isn't jewelry. She was smarter than that. Mean, but smart was the way she rolled."

Opening the first box, he turned it upside down. Empty. "Hmm. What would be the point of that?"

"Don't know. What's in the other one?"

He opened it. It was also empty. "This is really bizarre." Jacob turned it around and felt along it. He handed it to Maggie. "Check this out. Feel along that top section."

Maggie took it and, sure enough, along the top lining was something bumpy. She pulled the fabric away. It was a key. "Looks like a safe deposit box key."

"I wonder if anything else is in this one." Jacob held up the other one. "Want me to see?"

"Yeah, why not? It couldn't hurt."

Fumbling around, he eventually was able to free a slip of paper. He opened it and read it out loud. "'Ha, ha. Got you. You'll never find that diamond.'" He stared across the room at Maggie. "Did we just learn about a motive other than just her being a hateful women that many wanted to see dead?"

"Maybe so. I don't ever recall her wearing or owning any particularly nice jewelry when I saw her often. I also feel pretty sure if she had owned something worth a lot, she wouldn't have been able to keep from bragging about it."

"Someone obviously knew about it and was looking for it for Drusilla to go to all this trouble." Jacob pulled a couple of plastic evidence bags from his pocket. "Let's bag it all and see if we can get someone to analyze the writing to see if it's hers and get on the search for what bank that key could belong to. When we know, we'll need a warrant."

"Maybe the diamond is in there." Maggie bagged the box and key she held. She smacked herself in the forehead. "Gee. I didn't even think of handwriting analysis on that note we found on Drusilla's body. We need to get that one done, too."

"I already sent that on for testing."

"And didn't tell me?"

"Sorry," Jacob shrugged, "thought I did."

"Nope." She crossed her arms and stared at her partner. "Any other things you've done on *our* investigation that you haven't told me about?"

"What's the matter with you? Why are you mad at me?"

"I don't know. I'm overwhelmed with this case, I guess. It's a puzzle, and it seems every step we take sends us on another crazy tangent. I'm just tired of it all. Then I find out you're doing things I normally think to do myself."

Jacob stepped over and pulled her into a hug. "It's not a problem if you want to step aside. I know you said you could deal with the fact that you knew the victim, but if it seems to be overwhelming you, there's no shame in saying so. As you know, I had to step out on the investigation of Linus Anthony."

"Yeah, but that was your *wife*. This is merely someone I used to consider a friend." Maggie moved away from Jacob. "Come on. We have work to do. No need in moping around worrying that I'm not up to par. I'll get through it."

They rode back to the station in silence. Maggie's

brain was swirling. All the evidence and statements they'd taken were fighting for space in her head as she tried to sort through everything. Her left eye twitched.

Jacob glanced over at her. "I can almost hear those wheels turning. What conclusions have you come to?"

"None yet but I think we need to draw some things on the white board. Try to make sense of all the craziness coming at us."

"Let's do it," Jacob said. Inside the bullpen, he tossed her a red Dry Erase marker. "You do red, I'll do blue."

Maggie pulled copies of photos of the main players in Drusilla Issacs's life out of the file. She hung each with a clip, and Jacob came behind her to put their names underneath each one.

"Need to put Linus Anthony up here, too. I'm not sure how he relates to Drusilla, but somehow, he does. It would be too weird and coincidental if he didn't." Maggie nodded in Jacob's direction. "And you know I don't believe in coincidences."

"That I *do* know." Jacob used his marker to draw a diamond on the board with a question mark beside it.

"While I'm making the notes in red, how about running a copy of that safe deposit box key and sending it to all the banks to see if it's one of theirs. Starting with her normal banking institute which we have records of here." Maggie tapped the file.

She worked on the board, putting up the parts of each interview she deemed important.

By the time Jacob returned, the white surface was covered in red marker with arrows going from one suspect or witness to others.

"Wow. You've been busy," Jacob said, waving his paper around. "Ready to head to the courthouse with me to get this warrant signed to peek at a safe deposit box in First State Bank?"

"That was easy. You narrowed it down already?"

"Yep. Three calls was all it took." He grinned. "And interestingly, it wasn't at a bank we have any records for. All her other accounts were referred to in various files in her office. Wonder why she went elsewhere for this."

"Obviously to keep it secret. Especially if she didn't visit it often."

"See? You *do* know what you're doing. Never doubt yourself, Mags."

"While we're gone, we need to get Winslow and Stutsman in here to add to the board based on their interview with Linus. Are they in yet?" Maggie asked.

"Haven't seen them today." Jacob glanced around. "Captain Bone is in her office. I'll go update her while you call and see when they're expected in and let them know what we need."

Maggie nodded and pulled out her cell phone to call Stutsman.

e⁊oc⁊

They obtained a warrant signed by the duty judge and headed to First State Bank on Main Street.

After a discussion with the bank president and him calling his lawyer to be sure he had to comply with the warrant, Maggie and Jacob were led to an area on the far right of the bank, passing through a barred zone and into a room full of varying sizes of lockers.

The president led them to one of the medium size ones. He inserted his key and had Maggie insert Drusilla's.

Once they'd each turned their keys, he withdrew his. "You can go into any of the smaller rooms in this area. When you're done, I'll come back and we'll lock it up again."

Maggie nodded her thanks and pulled the box out of the wall. She and Jacob went into the closest room. She could barely stand waiting long enough to close the door to open the hinged lid.

Sitting down with Jacob beside her, she looked inside.

Jacob let out a low whistle. "Holy cow. What exactly was this woman into?"

Hands shaking, Maggie reached in and pulled out two gold bars. She hefted one in her hand. "These are heavy. I can only imagine how much one is worth. If they're solid gold."

"Oh, I'd bet they are. Let's count them." Jacob pulled them out one at a time. "Twelve. Wow. I'd sure like to know exactly what gold is selling for per ounce."

"Who are her heirs besides that husband of hers, Curtis Beane?" Maggie asked.

"Her parents, I think. She had no children so I would imagine if Beane killed her, these would go to them."

"This is plenty of motive for murder, isn't it?" Maggie reached into the box again and pulled out two velvet pouches.

"*Half* of one would be for some people, as we well know. Do you think Beane knew about these? I'm thinking not. Especially based on that house they lived in. It wasn't anything spectacular."

"No. It sure wasn't." Maggie still couldn't believe the amount of wealth in front of her. "Let's see what's in these pouches." She opened the first one and reached inside. "Feels like rocks."

"Flip them out on the table." Jacob patted the wood.

Maggie gently turned the bag on its side and allowed the contents to spread out on the surface. She let out a gasp. "What in the world?"

"Looks like another fortune in gemstones." Jacob picked up a red stone. "This is the biggest ruby I've ever seen."

"What are the others? I'm not much of a jewelry expert."

"Looks like mostly rubies and emeralds with maybe

a couple of sapphires." He picked up a black stone. "Look here. This is what's called a black star sapphire. Turn it slightly, and you can see what looks like a star in the middle."

Maggie took it from him and inspected it. "That's lovely. I wonder why she didn't try to have some of these set into necklaces or rings. She was always wearing jewelry. I can't imagine she'd be happy leaving these hidden here."

"Maybe they weren't really hers."

"I think you're right. That would be the only thing I could think of, too."

"There's one more pouch. Can your heart take one more reveal?" Jacob laughed as he tossed the packet in the air.

"I'm thinking that one has to be the diamond Drusilla referred to in that note we found in her drawer."

"Feels like more than one to me." Jacob turned the bag inside out, and four diamonds fell into his hand.

Maggie peered down at them. "They don't seem very big, so I wonder what that note meant. Maybe there's another one somewhere else. A bigger one."

"These may not be huge, but they look nice. We'll have to get a jeweler to assess them."

Pulling out her notepad, she nodded. "Best thing we can do now is an inventory. If we're going to take these out of here, we need to call the captain to come over. We don't want anyone questioning what we do with these."

"Good plan. I'll call her."

While they waited for Captain Bone to arrive, they sat still, each lost in their own thoughts.

Eventually, Maggie said, "I wonder if Drusilla somehow got involved with organized crime. I mean, really, how else could she have come into possession of all this stuff? It's way too valuable for her to have afforded it. Even the best accountant in the world couldn't afford to purchase these."

"Maybe in the world but surely not in small town America."

A knock on the door alerted them to the arrival of someone—hopefully the captain—with all this wealth on the table, they sure didn't want it to be anyone else.

Jacob stood and opened the door a crack, then all the way.

Captain Bone walked in. Her eyes opened wide. "Boy, you weren't lying, were you?"

Jacob grinned. "I've never lied to you, Captain."

"Okay, maybe not lie, but you *have* exaggerated in the past." The captain pulled up a chair. "Let's get this inventoried and back to the safe at the station. I have a couple of uniforms out there who will escort me back to the station with it in their cruiser."

"Good plan, boss." Jacob called out the items as Maggie wrote them down under the captain's watchful eye.

When they were finished, the captain asked, "How

do you two think our victim came by all of this?"

"We were just wondering that ourselves. We think she may have gotten sideways with organized crime." Maggie picked up the box in order to return it to the slot where it belonged. Something shifted inside.

"If she got in trouble with that sector of society, they wouldn't have played around with the manner of death. It would've been a headshot and game over," the captain said.

"Hang on a second, there's still something in here." Maggie sat the box down and turned it to face her. She leaned it upward to see what else could be inside.

It was a bundle of paper. Maggie pulled it out and handed it to the captain. She opened her notebook again and prepared to add this to the inventory.

Captain Bone unfolded the papers. Her eyes scanned the pages.

Maggie thought she would explode with anticipation before the captain told them what she was reading.

"Is it a confession?" Jacob asked.

"Not quite. Just some receipts."

"Showing she bought these items?" Maggie asked.

"No. For some gold coins. Krugerrands."

"Are those the kind we took from David Isaacs?" Jacob asked Maggie.

She nodded. "I think so." She turned to the captain. "May I see?"

Captain Bone handed Maggie the papers. "Sure."

Reading the receipts for herself, Maggie thought perhaps they were the coins Drusilla's ex-husband tried to take from her house. "I wonder why she kept the proof of purchases here but the coins in that Crown Royal bag in her house."

"Maybe she needed the money for something and took them out. Perhaps we should get the records from the bank for her visits. I know they can't tell us if she took anything out as they don't monitor that, but we can at least see when the last time she was in was. If it was this week, it could help us with the investigation." Jacob took the receipts from Maggie and looked them over himself.

"And if it was months ago, chances are, the coins have nothing to do with her death," Maggie said.

"Or they still could, and she was able to keep them hidden in her house longer than we suspect she would've needed to." The captain laid down a bag she'd brought with her. "Let's load this and get it back to the station."

"When we do, I'll get to work on the warrant for the records here," Jacob said.

"Good plan. I'd send for crime scene to see if there are other prints on this box, but I don't think we need to since these are monitored pretty closely." Finished with the loading of the bag, the captain stood. "I'll see you both at the station. Be sure to tell the bank president we'll let him know when we're ready to release the box so it can be rented again."

"I'll tell him on the way out," Jacob said.

After the captain left, they returned the empty box to its slot and stopped at the president's office to let him know they wanted him to keep the box under Drusilla's name a bit longer.

As they were leaving, Maggie handed him her card. "Call and let me know if anyone comes by and wants in the box."

"I will. So far, you're the only ones. Maybe her family members don't know about its existence. We usually get the heirs in almost before the coffin is interred."

"Sadly, there's a lot of greed out there, isn't there?" Maggie said.

The president shrugged. "Makes the world go round."

"We're getting a warrant to obtain the records of when Drusilla came by to visit the box. If you can gather that information in the next day or so, that would be helpful," Jacob said.

"I'll have someone go through the log and send it over as soon as the warrant arrives." The president turned in his chair to glance at his computer screen. "Is there anything else? I have some emails that need my attention."

"Nope. We're done." Jacob turned and walked out, followed by Maggie.

Back at the station, Maggie sat in front of the dry erase board for a long time, mulling over all the notations and photographs.

Something was niggling at the back of her mind, but she couldn't quite make the connection of what it was. Maybe something someone said or did? What was it? It was just out of reach. She focused so hard on trying to figure it out, when someone touched her shoulder, she let out a little squeal and leapt a bit in her chair.

Jacob laughed. "Whoa. I'm glad your weapon is hanging on the back of your chair. I could've lost some valuable body part."

Maggie's heart rate slowed to normal. "Didn't your mamma ever tell you not to sneak up on people?"

"Nope. She was always pranking people so she liked to scare us." Jacob winked. "Look, it's dark outside, we've been here all day, and I think we should go eat. Shift's been over."

"Then let's go." She grabbed her shoulder holster with her gun still in it and slid it on. "I'm making myself crazy looking at this board and trying to figure out what I missed."

The phone rang on Maggie's desk.

"Let someone else get it. I'm starving," Jacob said, jangling his keys.

Maggie couldn't do that. She wasn't wired that way. Holding up her left hand to halt his movement, she grabbed the receiver with her right. "Blaine." She listened for a few minutes. "We're on the way. Sit tight. Uniforms will be there before us since you called dispatch." She hung up.

"So much for my dinner, huh?" Dejected, Jacob's shoulders slumped.

"Got that right. Come on." Maggie led the way on their way to the parking lot. Almost at a run.

CHAPTER 11

They arrived quickly at Drusilla's office. Several cruisers were in front of the building and some officers were searching the perimeter.

Maggie glanced in the direction of Hattie's house. The old woman was on the porch, and it looked like John Hays was with her. Maggie shook her head at them and pointed toward Hattie's door. They went inside.

Walking over to the closest officer, Maggie asked, "Did you find anyone?"

"Nope. We found a couple of shoeprints and a couple of cigarette butts. We've bagged those for the CSI team. What dummy doesn't know not to leave that kind of thing in the bushes when there's been a crime?"

"Was anything taken?"

"Not that we can tell, but there's a broken window and some glass inside. Couple of guys cleared the building, but we're waiting for crime scene to go in and check for evidence."

"I guess the lady across the street called it in?"

"Nope. It was a man. He said he and his friend were grilling outside and heard a car pull in and then squeal off. They weren't sure what was happening so came around the house to see someone in a hoodie and jeans over here in the bushes."

"Grilling?" Jacob put his nose in the air and sniffed. "Ahh, yes. Food. I smell it."

"Will you stop it? You'll get fed as soon as we can get out of here." Maggie turned back to the officer. "But you didn't find anyone in there?"

"Like I said, nope, we didn't see anyone. Nada."

"Okay. Thanks. We'll be over talking to the witnesses if you need us. Page me when CSI gets here. I'd like to know what they find." Maggie turned to Jacob. "Come with me. Maybe you can cadge a burger or something. Hattie likes to feed people."

"I'm in." Jacob laughed. "And of course, the most important thing is getting those witness statements."

"Of course." Maggie trotted across the road and knocked on Hattie's door.

When John answered, Maggie said, "You two needed to stay inside. You don't know who was over there or what they were capable of doing."

"Lady, I was in combat. I'm not going to hide from anyone." John smiled as if to ease the way he spoke to her, but she wasn't buying it.

"I know you were, but I worry about Hattie. She's not able to fight off someone who may have murder on his mind. Someone broke Drusilla's neck, and if that was the same person who was over there tonight, that could've turned out badly."

John placed an arm on Hattie's shoulders. "I'm not about to let anyone hurt her."

Hattie pushed on him playfully. "You're saying that because you like my cake."

"I like you, too, woman. Not just your cooking skills," John said.

Hattie grinned. "I'm old enough to be your mamma."

"Not quite and who says the man always has to be older than the woman?" John pulled her closer and actually kissed the top of her head.

The way they'd taken to each other made Maggie's heart happy. Even if she never solved this case, she at least had brought two lonely souls together, and that was pretty cool in her book.

"You two are adorable, but you need to stay out of harm's way. Sticking to the inside of the house is the safest bet. For now, we're waiting on the crime scene techs to check the bushes over there to see if they missed anything. For someone to be in the bushes this evening after we searched the premises again today is very suspicious."

Maggie took hold of the screen door. "Let's go in and wait for news of what they find."

"We have plenty of food. Come on in and eat with us," John said.

"You don't have to ask me twice." Jacob was right behind John. "When we're on a case like this, we can't eat regularly, and I think it's actually been several days since I had a meal."

"Hey, Hattie, where's Mordecai?" Maggie asked.

"I don't know. That little devil took off earlier today and hasn't come back. I'm a little worried as he usually gets hungry before now and makes his way to the food bowl." Hattie showed them into the kitchen.

On the table was a feast of meats and vegetables. There were ribs, burgers, chicken, and even a brisket. There was also a pile of corn on the cob, some beans, and a bowl of potatoes.

"Good grief, were you expecting a crowd?" Maggie asked as she took a seat.

"I always like to cook a lot while I have the grill hot. This is going to last several days." John pulled out a chair for Hattie and then for himself. "It makes the best use of the coals since I like a real charcoal fire."

Jacob served himself some vegetables and grabbed a hamburger bun. "It sure smells good."

A scratching at the kitchen door startled Maggie. Her hand went immediately to her gun.

Hattie stood.

"Wait, we don't know who that is. Don't open the door." Maggie brushed past Hattie and put her ear to the door.

"It's going to be Mordecai, Miss Maggie. He comes to that door when he wants food."

"Let me check it out first." Maggie didn't hear anything for a moment, then the scratching noise started again, accompanied by a plaintive mewling sound. Yep. It was the cat.

She opened the door, and Mordecai came strolling in. He had something in his mouth and dropped it beside his food bowl as he started in on the kibble.

"Did that scoundrel bring in another toad or lizard? He's always bringing me presents." Hattie knelt beside the animal. After a moment, she stared up at Maggie. "Come look at this."

Maggie squatted at her side. She peered at the item Mordecai brought in. "I'm not sure what that is. It looks like it's made of Lycra or some other stretchy material. I'm wondering if we should bag it and tag it for the crime scene unit. They may be able to tell us what it is. Who knows, Mordecai could've gotten it from across the street."

"I don't know, but if you think you should have it tested, I think the cat will get over losing his pretty toy."

"If not, we can bring him a new one tomorrow if you make us lunch," Jacob said with a laugh. He pulled an evidence bag out of his pocket and passed it to Maggie. "You sure it's not a rubber?"

"Hush. No, it isn't. It's red." Maggie shook her head at his crazy comment.

Jacob laughed again. "You've led a sheltered life, Mags, if you've never seen a colored prophylactic."

John spread his hands to indicate the spread of food on the table. "Not to change the very intriguing conversation, but lunch is made. Just come by any time."

"Watch out, he *will* take you up on that," Maggie said. Her pager went off. She checked the number. "Looks like the crime scene folks are here. I'll walk this over." Maggie dangled the baggie.

"Want me to come with you?" Jacob asked.

"No. You go on and feed your face. I can handle it."

She headed across the street and met James in the yard.

"We're going to search the bushes since that's where the person in the hoodie was spotted, but I have to say, I thought we got everything the day of the murder when we searched then." He crossed his arms. "Makes me wonder if someone was over here planting something. You know, since we came out today. Maybe whoever it was thinks the neighbors are watching the place and this was a chance to plant something to throw off the investigation."

"Or maybe there was something there, and a cat found it." She waggled the bag at him. "Run a test on this while you're testing, please."

James raised his eyebrows. "A cat brought you that?"

"Yep. To the cake lady across the street. He brings her prizes."

He laughed. "That's interesting."

Angela, the other crime scene tech came, over. "Just found this, Detective Blaine." She held up a baggie with a cigarette butt in it.

"Yeah, right. Where was it?" she asked.

"Under the window right near the front of the victim's office."

James stared at Maggie for a moment. Together they both said, "Planted."

"For sure it was. We'd have found it on that first search. Want to put down a wager on who's DNA we'll find?" James asked.

Maggie shrugged. "Nope, because at this moment I don't even know if any of our suspects smoke. I haven't been looking for that evidence."

James waggled his brows. "I know who smokes."

"You do? Who?"

"The secretary does. She had several packs in her drawer as well as breath mints, breath spray, and even a fancy lighter. I also believe the husband smokes because there was a lighter on the victim's desk as well. It had initials engraved on the side. Same first and last initial as the husband."

"Was there a middle initial?"

"Yep. It was a B."

"Then that's him. His middle name is Brian. Well done on catching that." Maggie tapped the bag she held. "I think we're more likely to get a lead off this. Remember though, when you're testing it, that it has kitty DNA on it since he was toting it in his mouth."

"And we have no idea how long he's had it since we can't very well interrogate the witness, can we?"

"We could, but he would either take the fifth and remain silent or merely purr in your face."

"Yep. That could be a problem." James pointed to the van he arrived in. "Heading to the lab now. There wasn't much else to find."

"Did you get the tests run on the powders you found?"

"Not yet but close. We're also still checking out the Red Bull cans we found in the trash out back."

"Let me know what you find. No matter what time it is. I'd like to move this along and get the body to her family so they can bury her. I know her parents. They're quite nice. Too bad they had such bad luck with one of their children."

"Yeah. I can only imagine how it is to have your child die in such a horrible way."

Maggie nodded. She wasn't about to tell this man she'd known for a couple of days that what she meant was Drusilla's sister and brother were nice people but Drusilla wasn't. She'd somehow become an unkind, conniving, unethical woman, even though she was raised by a church going, loving family. It always mystified Maggie when one kid in a clan went bad and the others led normal lives. Sometimes she regretted not going into psychology as it did intrigue her so.

"Be sure to call me as soon as you can. Like I said, I want to call her parents to let them know when they can claim her body."

"So, not going to release her to the next of kin?"

"Yeah, well, technically, I have to unless I get the goods on him, don't I?"

"You think it's him then?" James held the baggies in one hand and ran his other across his face.

"He's involved. I'm sure of it. My gut doesn't lie. I can't prove it yet, and I'm not sure how deep he is in it, but trust me, he is."

"All right." He nodded. "I'm off to the lab. We're going to get this done by the end of the week, okay?"

"Sounds good." She turned to walk back to Hattie's place.

"And then you'll let me take you to dinner?"

Stunned at the invitation, Maggie didn't know what to say. Sure, he was attractive, but she hadn't thought about dating anyone in ages. She sure hadn't had any designs on the handsome new guy.

In fact, if she thought about it at all, she realized she thought he was probably involved with someone. Why wouldn't he be?

"We'll see about that," she said over her shoulder.

Back at Hattie's, she noticed the woman seated on the porch in the dark. "Where are John and Jacob?"

"They said they'd clean up the kitchen so I came out to watch you talking to that tall man who seems to be smitten with you. I heard him ask you to dinner. You're going to say no, aren't you?"

"It's quite likely." Maggie made a face. "I haven't dated in a long time, and it seems to be a lot of hassle."

"You're never gonna get you a man with that attitude."

"Maybe I don't want one." Maggie plopped down in the chair next to Hattie's. "I like my not-messy life. Men cause problems. They want, they need, they have to have—"

Hattie patted Maggie's knee. "Someone hurt you bad, didn't they?"

"What makes you think that?"

"Honey, you make me think that. Those words you just spoke about men. They tell me a lot."

"How about you and John then?" Desperate to change the subject, Maggie asked about the veteran. "He seems to want to date you. What are you going to say? Yes?"

"Don't think I don't know what you're doing. You want to make me talk about my friendship with John, so I will leave you alone about that man who wants to take you to dinner."

"You really are too smart for your own good." Maggie reached over and squeezed Hattie's hand. "I appreciate your concern about me, but I'll be fine."

"You'll end up like me if you don't watch out. I do at least have kids—don't see them often enough—but it's mostly just me, Mordecai, and the television. Trust me, you don't want to be an old lady alone and lonely. It's a hard way to live, Detective."

"I hope things are changing for you. You have a new friend in me as well as John. I don't plan to solve this case and then disappear from your life. I want us to stay friends. You're fun to be around, and I enjoy the time I've had with you."

"That's sweet, hon, but I also want you to find romance and love in your life."

"I don't need that. Been there." She smiled ruefully at the older woman. "Protecting myself is vital for me right now. I don't have any desire to get muddied up in a relationship at the moment."

Hattie shook her head and opened her mouth to say something else, but the screen door opened.

Jacob stepped onto the porch, followed by John. "Ready to go, Mags? We still have a couple of things to take care of before we can call it a night."

She stood. "Yeah. We do."

When they were on the grass, Maggie waved. "We'll see you soon. Be safe and stay inside. Don't be going over to the crime scene. It seems to be a hot bed of activity so I'd prefer you keep away."

"We'll try, Maggie, but you know how Hattie can be. I'll keep an eye on her," John said.

"Thanks again for dinner," Jacob said.

They headed back to the station. Jacob whistled under his breath.

Maggie hadn't heard him whistle since his wife died. It was odd to have him do so now, especially since they'd just found her murderer.

"You're in a good mood," Maggie said.

"It's amazing what good food and good company will do for you." He placed a hand on hers where it lay on the seat. "And a good night's sleep. First in a very long time."

Glad it was dark in the car, Maggie ducked her head as the heat suffused her cheeks. That good night's sleep he spoke of was in her bed, spooned against her back.

೮ාඓ

The next morning, Maggie awoke alone and found she kind of missed having Jacob beside her. Weirded out by that thought, she rose, hurriedly took her shower, and fastened her weapon into her shoulder holster.

At the station, they made their way to the lab to see if there were any results on any of their evidence. James was off duty, but a guy named Chen was there, and he told them the results on the piece of Lycra.

"It was definitely Lycra. It had feline DNA as well as DNA from an unknown donor. Someone not in the databases. There's hope for a match if you find a suspect."

"Was it like a bathing suit or bra or what?" Jacob asked.

"My money is on bodybuilding fabric. You know, the outfits those people who bulk up and show their muscles wear?"

"What makes you think that?" Maggie asked.

"Because it's the right texture and weight. I've got one of the other techs tracking down where the fabric came from. Where it would be sold. Dye lot and all that jazz."

"Let us know when you nail it down more." Jacob tapped his index finger on the countertop. "I guess we're going to look for a bodybuilder now. The victim's former husband works at a gym. Better start there, huh?"

"Let's go." Maggie led the way down the hall and to the parking lot. "I have a feeling David is going to love seeing us again, now that he's out on bail. It always kills me that as soon as we lock them up, they have someone dash right out to the bondsman and pay their ten percent so they can be back on the streets."

"Who do you think it will be? I haven't seen anyone who would qualify as a bodybuilder in our list of suspects. In fact, most of them don't seem to be the kind to work out at all. Even the ex-husband who runs the gym seems a bit of a slacker to me," Jacob said.

"No room to talk here. Neither of us are gym rats." Maggie drove this time, even though she preferred to leave that to her partner.

"I like a woman with softness to her. Those bony women or the ones who are all muscles aren't appealing to me at all. Give me a lady who has curves and her own home-grown breasts any day over those other gals."

She eyed him sideways and let out a snort. "Home grown breasts?"

"You know exactly what I mean."

Shaking her head, she pulled into the parking lot at the gym. "Come on, Mr. Boob Expert and let's see if we can see if our friend David knows any body builders."

"You know, there are a lot more gyms in town than this one. Who knows who the person was who had on that Lycra suit? He or she could be from anywhere."

"I realize that but we have to start somewhere, don't we? Might as well be this place since we *do* know one person who hangs out here who knows our victim well enough to want to kill her."

"So you think there may be a kill Drusilla club that meets here?" Jacob held the glass door open for Maggie to enter.

"It certainly isn't among the impossible things in life. I mean, really, how many people do you know who had to be killed four ways?"

"There's always Rasputin. Didn't it take like eight ways to get that guy?"

"You a history buff now or something?" she asked with a grin.

"Or something."

They stepped inside. Once her eyes adjusted to the change in lighting, Maggie glanced around, trying to locate David.

A woman in a skin-tight black pair of shorts and a cropped sweatshirt that showed off taut abs walked over. "I'm Stacey. Can I help you?"

"We're looking for David. Is he around?"

Stacey jerked her thumb toward the back wall. "He's back there greasing up Tabitha. He got a new brand oil, and they're testing it."

"Greasing?" Jacob asked.

"Yeah. Go on back. They won't mind. Through the green door. The tanning booths are back there, too." She looked Maggie up and down. "You might want to book some time in there. You're too pale."

Maggie ignored her and headed to the green door. Jacob was right behind her. "Don't you listen to her. You're just the right amount of pale."

Over her shoulder, she said, "Remind me to punch your lights out when we get out of here."

"I'll make a note of it."

She opened the door and reeled back at the sight in front of her. "Ugh." The word came out unbidden.

Jacob pushed past her and exhaled. "With the right woman, maybe…"

Maggie pushed him slightly. "Hush."

David looked up from his task of slathering some kind of greasy substance on the woman in front of him. "What the hell are you doing here? What's wrong with you people? I told you, I had nothing to do with Drusilla's death."

"We have some more questions we'd like to ask. It won't take long." Maggie nodded at the woman covered in oil. "You can continue in a minute. All we want to know is if there are any bodybuilders at this gym that knew your former wife."

"Sure there were. When we were married, she was around a lot. She worked out here so, yeah, people knew her."

"Any in particular?" Jacob asked.

The greasy woman Stacey had called Tabitha spoke before David could. "Sure, if you're looking for someone who didn't like Drusilla. It would be Linda Matthews."

Jacob pulled out his notebook. "Who's she?"

"Dammit, Tabs. Why the hell did you say that?" David practically foamed at the mouth.

This was interesting. Maggie was even more curious now that David was making it a big deal.

Tabitha shook her head as if she wasn't intimidated by David. "Listen, this is the cops, Dave. We don't mess with the law in my family. They need to know about Linda. She hated your wife, first for stealing her husband and then that kid."

"Shut up. You're only sending them after her because she usually wins at your competitions, and you want her to be a suspect so she can't come to the one this weekend." David pressed the oily stuff onto Tabitha's legs as if he wanted to rub it in all the way to the bone.

"Let go. You're hurting me," Tabitha said.

"Perhaps you should return to your office, David, until we get done here." Maggie opened the door and tilted her head toward the main gym floor. She definitely wanted to talk to him about the gems they'd found, but she also wanted to hear what Tabitha had to say.

"I manage this place. You can't toss me out of my own premises."

"Watch us haul you in to the station again right now if you don't go." Jacob pulled his cuffs from where they hung at his back. "How will it go down for your customers to see you hauled out of here? You want to play it that way, it's fine with me. I kind of like making jerks look like who they really are to the people around them. You know, the ones who are fooled into thinking you might be a good guy?"

"I'm going, but be sure it's only because I plan to call your chief or captain or whatever and report your conduct."

"Good. Please do. Her name is Captain Bone. Give her my regards." Jacob grinned. "Spelled like it sounds. B-O-N-E."

David stomped out of the area. As soon as he was

gone, Maggie closed the door and turned to Tabitha. "What can you tell us about this Linda Matthews and Drusilla?"

"Linda's a bodybuilder like me, and we've known each other a long time as we compete against each other. She was involved with Curtis before he hooked up with Drusilla. They had a kid, but he didn't want to get married. He was fine with being that boy's daddy, but he's a player and didn't want to commit to Linda. She kept holding on to hope that he'd marry her."

"But he didn't and married Drusilla instead? That made her hate Drusilla?" Maggie asked.

Tabitha wiped her hands on a towel. "It didn't quite happen that way. Drusilla and Curtis met on a dating site. He saw the kind of money she made and latched on to her. She always paid wherever they went, and he was digging that. Linda was upset with him, but he told her he wasn't really interested in Drusilla but what she could get for him. The circles she moved in were tempting."

"But eventually, he did dump Linda, right?" Maggie asked.

"Nope. I don't think he ever really did. I mean, yeah, he married that witch, but only because she told him if he didn't, she would toss him out of her house. By then, he'd let his own go, and Linda wouldn't let him live with her since he was sleeping with them both as well as a couple of other women I heard about. He's truly a snake."

"Sounds like it." Maggie could hardly take in the

news about the man. Sure, she'd always thought he wasn't quite the caliber of man for Drusilla—especially when they were friends—but she had no idea he was such a low life.

Jacob looked up from his pad where he'd been scribbling notes. "Do you think this Linda would be capable of harming Drusilla?"

"I can't say, but she's very strong from all the body building so she could do some damage to someone if she wanted to." Tabitha rubbed her legs until they shone. "How do you like this new oil? It seems to really show my muscles to great effect." She flexed and posed.

Maggie couldn't resist a glance at her partner. She almost laughed at his barely repressed shudder. It was true. The pose *was* a little off-putting.

"Do you have an address for Linda?" Maggie asked.

"Yeah. I don't know it off my head, but I can tell you how to get to her place."

"That's fine. I'll jot the directions." Jacob flipped a page and waited for her to tell him.

Tabitha thought for a few minutes then rattled it off.

When they arrived at Linda's home, Maggie led the way to the front door. She stood to the side while Jacob knocked.

When a blonde woman with super-short hair and a physique that clearly belonged to a body builder opened the door, she took a step back and made a move as if to close the door.

Jacob put his foot in the way so she couldn't. "Police department. Are you Linda Matthews?"

She nodded then ducked her head as if she regretted admitting it.

He whipped out his badge and showed it to her. "Got a few minutes?"

"I don't know nothing about nothing, and I have somewhere I need to be. I was on my way out."

"Funny." Jacob nodded at her shirt and bare feet. "Without your pants and shoes?"

"I meant in a few minutes."

Maggie stepped around so the woman could see her. "Then we promise to only take a few since you obviously have a little window of time."

"I really don't, and you can't make me let you in or talk to you." Linda jutted out her chin and glared at Maggie.

"You're right that I can't enter your house without a warrant, but I sure can take you to the station to have a conversation. That will delay you more than the few moments we're asking to have." Maggie jerked her head toward Jacob. "Wanna cuff her and put her in the car?"

Linda threw her hands in the air in surrender. "Good grief. Just ask what you want to know here on my porch, but I don't know nothing."

Maggie wanted to laugh at the number of double negatives the woman was tossing around but decided that wouldn't go far in getting any information out of her.

"Are you acquainted with Drusilla Isaacs?" Maggie asked with her pad and pencil out to make notes.

"You mean that baby-daddy stealing butch-looking woman?"

Not knowing quite how to respond to that since she'd never thought of Drusilla as masculine—especially with her massive breasts she liked to show inappropriately— Maggie stood stunned for a moment.

Jacob took up the slack. "If that's how you refer to the woman who has an accounting office on East Main Street, then yeah, that's who we mean."

"She stole my man and then even tried to steal my kid by calling herself his bonus mom. That heifer is not any kind of mom, and she certainly isn't a mother to Little Man."

"Your child's name is Little Man?" Maggie couldn't resist asking.

"His name is Curtis like his daddy, but we call him Little Man." She pushed her chest forward. "You got a problem with that?"

"No. Not at all. It just seemed odd the way you said Drusilla isn't a mother to Little Man."

"And she ain't. Never will be." She closed the door and stepped onto the porch.

"That much is true. I presume you know she's dead, right?" Jacob asked.

Linda's eyes widened. She let out a gasp and pressed

her hand to her chest. "You've got to be kidding me. No way. What happened?"

She wasn't fooling Maggie. The woman was clearly not an actress. She couldn't even fake shock at the death of the woman who she had every reason to hate. "Do you think we're idiots?"

"Of course not. I don't even know you, but if you show up on my porch and tell me a woman I don't like is dead, don't be thinking I'll be shedding a tear. I couldn't stand her when she was alive, and I sure don't care that she's dead. Nothing to do with me." Linda leaned back on the door, her bottom lip poked out.

"Can you understand that we'd want to discuss this matter with you? If Drusilla's husband is your child's father, you might have a motive to want her dead. Can you tell us where you were three afternoons ago?" Maggie pointed the end of her pencil at the woman.

"Right here. Watching TV. That's about all I ever do now that Curtis is married to that woman. He takes Little Man a lot so I'm left here alone."

"But sometimes he stays here with you and the child? Overnight, right?" Jacob asked.

A sly look slid across her face. "You know it. My man can't stay away."

"So you and Curtis were having an affair?" Maggie poised her pencil to get this down.

"It's only right, ain't it? She stole my man, I steal him back." The woman smiled, but it was more like a grimace. The expression on Linda's face was ugly and hateful—more than the face of someone who wasn't upset over a death, more like one who was part of the reason that the death happened—one that called for a deeper interrogation than on the front porch of her home.

Maggie resisted the urge to glance over at Jacob but presumed they were on the same page, as far as taking her in to question her more formally, when he said, "Please place your hands behind your back."

"What the hell for?" Linda spat the words out.

Jacob rattled the cuffs he'd taken out. "We're taking you in."

"For what?" Belligerent and angry, Linda reached behind her and turned the handle of her front door.

Before the woman could get inside and lock them out, Maggie lunged for her. The door opened in that moment, and Maggie fell forward, taking Linda down with her.

CHAPTER 12

Rubbing her sore hip where she hit the knob on Linda's door, Maggie hobbled along down the hallway at the precinct. "Let's let her stew in lockup for a while."

"And do what?" Jacob asked.

"Make some calls about the things we found in Drusilla's safe deposit box. Weren't we on the way to talk to someone about that when we got sidetracked by the body builder?"

"Yep. We were going to talk to David, the former husband, again."

She laughed. "He's going to love seeing us back at the gym for a third time, isn't he?"

"Almost makes me want to speed on the drive over."

The captain passed them on their way out. "What's going on? You dash in, drop off a woman I wouldn't want to get into a tussle with, and then dart back out into the parking lot?"

Jacob laughed. "Yeah, boss. She was a pit stop on the way to check on some of those jewels. Decided to leave her here for safekeeping until she gets good and tired of waiting. She's already in a pretty sour mood, so be sure to pop in and check on her to see if she needs some refreshment."

"I'll probably wait and let you do that since you seem to like her so much." Captain Bone smiled. "But don't leave it too long, okay?"

"We won't. We'll be back before you even realize we're gone," Jacob said.

When they returned to the gym, ready to try to pin David Isaacs down on what he knew about the gems and gold, Maggie's brain finally kicked in.

The thought that had been niggling at her brain since she'd sat in front of the whiteboard suddenly manifested itself.

She smacked her forehead with her hand. "Hang on a minute. I need to make a call."

"What? I see the wheels turning in your head."

"Something was eating at the back of mind for a while, almost since we found those gemstones. I think I finally figured it out."

Jacob leaned his arms on the steering wheel and

watched as she punched in a number on her phone. "Are you going to enlighten me?"

She held up her left index finger. "Listen." When James answered his phone, she said, "Hey, James, I just thought about something. Do you have Drusilla's gun handy there in the lab where you can get your hands on it quickly?"

Jacob looked as if he understood where she was going with her idea. His face lit up as if he did.

"Yeah, check those crystals in the handle of that gun. I have a feeling you're going to find that they aren't crystals at all but small real gemstones, including diamonds." She nodded her head. "That's what I'm thinking, yeah. Call me back when you know something."

She pushed the disconnect button. "If she was involved with our friend, Linus Anthony, and they had a falling out over the gems and gold, wouldn't he be ideal to be her murderer? After all, we know he has no compunction about killing."

"Yeah, but it seems a bit sloppy for him, and wouldn't he have tried to take a trophy from her as well?"

"Maybe he was interrupted and had to get away quickly."

"But do you think he'd use four methods to kill her?"

"I still think we may have more than one person involved, but just think, if Linus and Drusilla were partners in some illegal gem enterprise, he could very well have turned on her." Maggie snapped her fingers. "Or better yet, Drusilla hid those items in the safe deposit box to keep them from her partner, and he attacked her in a quest to find out where she hid them. It got out of hand, and he ended up killing her."

"Okay, okay. I concede you could be on to something. Let's see what they find in the lab when they look closer." He opened his door. "Let's go rattle David's chain and see if he has any info on whether Linus and Drusilla know each other or had any business dealings together."

As soon as they entered the gym, David came dashing over with a look of rage on his face. When he got within whispering distance, he hissed then said, "Get out of here. You can't keep coming around and harassing me. I'm going to call your supervisor."

Maggie entered the passcode on her phone and punched in the direct dial to Captain Bone. She passed the phone to David. "Here's my captain now. Go ahead and tell her whatever you want."

David stepped away from the phone and refused to take it.

"Sorry, boss. I thought Mr. Isaacs wanted to speak with you about Jacob's conduct, but he says, no, he's fine now." Maggie hung up.

Jacob poked her in the back. "You didn't have to toss me under that passing bus."

"We all know if anyone should be reported to the boss for something, it would be you." She laughed and faced David. "Got a few minutes for some old friends?"

"You think you're so smart. You're not funny at all, and I hope I live long enough to see you get what's coming to you." David stalked across the gym toward his office. "Do not open your mouth out here in the public area, or I *will* talk to your captain next time."

The man had already shown he was full of empty words, but just for fun Maggie asked, "Are you sure you want to say that you want me to get what's coming to me? That sounds like a threat against an officer of the law."

"You know as well as I do what I mean." He opened the door to his office and allowed her and Jacob to precede him into the room. When he slammed the door behind him, the glass in the top shuddered in such a way Maggie was afraid it would fall out of the framing.

David walked around his desk and sat in his chair. "Now what do you want? And please, try to ask everything you could ever possibly want to know about me and Dru before you leave. I don't want to see either of you here again."

"Even if I wanted to buy a three year membership?" Jacob asked with a grin.

"Even then." David leaned his chair against the wall. "Ask."

"Do you know a Linus Anthony?" Maggie asked with pen poised to take notes.

The front legs of David's chair hit the floor with a thud as it came down on the floor. "Who?"

"After that reaction, I don't think you can pretend you don't know the man," Jacob said. "What were your or Drusilla's dealings with him?"

"He was one of her accounting clients."

"That it?" Jacob raised his eyebrows.

David shrugged. "That's all I know."

"Try again." Maggie leaned forward and stared him in the eyes.

"You must think you have something."

"Oh, we do, and I suggest you share what you know before you find yourself in a lot of trouble. Since she's not here, we can only surmise what part you may have played in Drusilla's scheme." Maggie was totally bluffing but counted on the man not realizing it and saying enough to help them.

"Look. I might know something more, but I want immunity before I talk to you about it."

"What do you know about immunity?" Maggie asked.

"Just what I've seen on TV, but I want it, or I'm not saying anything."

"Tell you what, we can probably get the prosecutor's office on board for limited immunity on whatever you might have done with Linus Anthony and your former wife, but no way will we be able to agree to immunity if you had anything to do with Drusilla's death," Maggie said.

David waved his hand in a dismissive way. "I don't have to worry about that since I had nothing to do with her murder."

"All right then, tell us what you know about Drusilla and Linus Anthony," Maggie said.

"Don't you need to call someone about my immunity?"

"Sure. My partner will phone while you and I chat." Maggie nodded to Jacob. "Go on and make the call." After Jacob left the room, Maggie asked, "What do you know?"

"Shouldn't we wait until he comes back?"

"Tell you what, if he doesn't get the immunity permission, I won't use anything you say against you. Time is really of the essence here, and I'd like to get your statement and get out of here."

"You promise not to double cross me?"

Maggie held her hand up as if she were a Girl Scout. "On my honor."

He stared at her for a moment and must have liked what he saw in her eyes because he started to talk, "Dru met the guy when he came in to hire her to do a tax return. He said some friend of his recommended her. She thought he was a bit of a weirdo but when she quoted him her fee, he didn't hesitate and pulled out a wad of bills. Since he clearly could pay, she latched on to him."

"Something she did a lot?"

"Oh, yeah." David nodded. "Once she knew people had money, she would milk them for it. Weirdly, when we were married, I wanted us to get a better house with all the money she was making, but she was so obsessed with buying gold and coins that she wouldn't even consider leaving that neighborhood."

"It doesn't seem that bad to me. Sure the houses are older, but there's low crime there."

"She wanted kids in a really bad way. We'd started trying, but then I realized I didn't even like to be in the same room as her, and I had to get out."

"I'm confused. Was it her or the neighborhood?"

He slammed his hand on the table. "It was actually the house itself as well as her meanness. She would go along all nice and friendly and snuggle up to me like I could do no wrong and then, before I knew it, she was cold and making my life miserable. Way too much fighting and then silent treatment happened in that house. I asked her to sell and move so we could truly start over. She refused, I moved out."

"What did she do with all the gold and coins she was buying?"

"Hid them somewhere. Dru gave me some when we got divorced. I agreed to sign the house over to her within the last few months, but I wanted her to buy me out by giving me some of the Kruggerands. That's why I was at her house that day you found me. She'd promised them to me in exchange for the deed. I was stupid enough to sign the deed and trust her secretary to hold it until I got the coins."

"And she double crossed you by giving it to Drusilla. You never got paid."

"Right. That's why I was there that day. To find those coins."

"You had a motive to kill her, then." Maggie tapped her pen on his desk.

"But I didn't. That Linus guy had way more motive than I did. She started stealing from him almost as soon as he became her client."

"In what way?"

"He and she entered into some scheme with gemstones and diamonds. I don't know any details, but when they started, Dru and I were still married. She would bring home stones and say she was keeping them. For some reason, she thought the man wouldn't miss them. I wasn't so sure. He was a bit too creepy for me, and I tried to stay away from him."

Maggie couldn't agree more about the man being creepy. Maybe this ex-husband of Drusilla had more sense than she'd given him credit for.

Jacob reentered the small office. "We're a go on the limited immunity."

"Good. I'm glad." David wiped his brow. "Do you have what you need from me?"

"I think so. Thanks." Maggie stood. "We hope not to

have to return but remember, you did give me some in-formation that shows you had a motive in Drusilla's death so it's not over yet."

David's face flushed. "Hey, I thought if I cooperated with you that you'd leave me alone."

"Don't get bent about it. I was merely saying we *might* be back if we need to. I also said thanks, and I *do* mean that. You've answered some questions that help us, and we're truly appreciative and may even owe you if they result in a solution for this crime."

"I'm glad you're at least acknowledging it." David rose. "And I sincerely hope you never have to come here again."

"Us too." Maggie held her hand out to shake his. "Have a good rest of the day." She turned to Jacob. "Let's go. We have to see what our Mr. Linus Anthony is willing to share with us regarding some scheme he was involved in with our victim."

"Sounds intriguing. Can't wait." Jacob held the door open to allow her to pass.

"You have no idea."

∾∾∾

As soon as the corrections officer escorted Linus Anthony into the interrogation room, the prisoner raised his eyebrows and grinned in Maggie's direction. "I wondered when you were going to get back to me. Finally figured out some things?"

The officer pulled out the metal chair for the cuffed Linus then retreated to the outer vestibule to wait to take him to his cell.

"We *do* have some additional questions for you," Jacob said.

"I'm at your service. What can I help you detectives with?"

Maggie wanted to smack him. He was acting as if he were some kind of consultant having to educate the stupid. Of course, it didn't help that she did feel a bit dumb for not figuring out the so-called crystals on the gun may be tied to the gems in Drusilla's safe deposit box. Hadn't she always heard that old adage about hiding in plain sight?

"What can you tell us about your dealings with Drusilla and gemstones?" Maggie decided it was better to act as if they already knew. She was pretty sure David was telling the truth when he said Drusilla and the man had a deal to launder the money they would bring.

"Ahh, so you finally pulled her gun out of the evidence bag. I have to say, my beautiful detective, I thought you were smarter than you turned out to be. Bagging and tagging the firearm and placing it in the evidence room slowed you down some in your investigation didn't it? What made you finally decide there might be something there?" Linus nodded at Jacob. "Or did your sidekick come up with that idea? Was he intrigued by a woman who might be a bit more feminine than his partner? One who wanted a pretty weapon?"

Jacob made a move as if to go for Linus.

Maggie held her hand up to stop him. "Hang on a minute, Jacob. This arrogant piece of crap seems to forget where he is. He's here for the duration with everything we have on him."

Linus spread his cuffed hands on the table. "If you have so much on me, why should I even entertain the prospect of talking to you? I don't have to share what I know at all." He glanced around the room. "In fact, I don't see my lawyer here so I should probably clam up anyway."

"That's your right, but I think we *do* have something to offer you in exchange for your information," Maggie said.

"For info on my dealings with the treacherous Drusilla Isaacs or for info on her death?"

"How about both?" Jacob asked.

"It would take a mighty good deal for me to do that." He leaned back in the chair with a smug, self-satisfied smile.

Trying to suppress her excitement at his words that he may know about Drusilla's death, Maggie made herself sit still for a moment as if thinking over his words. Finally, she said, "In exchange for the scoop on your dealings with her while she was alive, how about we allow you some additional privileges? Both here and in the prison you end up in?"

"What would those be, dear? And you *do* know you have to convict me first, right?"

"I'm well aware of that, but that's not going to be a problem. We have you in so many ways, you really have no bargaining power."

"There you go again, saying things that make me want to stay silent." Linus turned to Jacob. "Perhaps you can tell the little lady here that her interrogation skills need some work. She's supposed to make friends with me to convince me she's on my side. She's doing it wrong."

Not taking the bait, Maggie said, "It really doesn't matter if you help us or not. We'll still figure out what happened to Drusilla." She was taking a chance but if he really was a classic narcissist as Doctor McDaniel said, he wouldn't be able to resist taunting them with what he knew. After all, he ended up in their custody in the first place because he couldn't stop himself from calling them.

"You'll never finesse it. It's really kind of a beautiful thing that happened to her. Well-deserved, I must say." Another sly grin passed over Linus' face. "Never seen a woman so young, yet hated by so many."

"Let's get back to your actual dealings with her, can we?" Jacob asked.

"Sure. You're lead man on this. What do you want to know?" The chains on Linus's cuffs rattled against the edge of the table.

Jacob had his pen and pad out. "How did you meet her and when?"

"I needed an accountant. Some dude I know told me to call her."

"Who was that?" Jacob asked.

"Don't remember, man. I just remember being at a party and asking around. Some dude said to go to her."

"Because she was a good accountant?" Jacob continued and Maggie decided to let him take the lead while she watched for reactions on the prisoner's face.

Linus let out a laugh. "Oh, hell no. That wasn't it at all."

"Then what did this dude tell you about her that led you to her office?"

"That she had large breasts, and she liked to show them off. What man could resist that?" Linus snickered. "Pretty good marketing plan, don't you think? You know, 'come let me do your taxes, and I'll give you a peek at my goodies.'"

Maggie couldn't let that pass by. She'd long wondered about Drusilla and her too-tight clothes. "And did she actually do that? Pull them out and show to you?"

"Why, dearie? Do you want to show me yours and let me tell you they are better than hers?" He eyeballed Maggie's chest. "You look a bit puny compared to her, but those big ones begin to sag too soon." Shaking his head, he added, "Alas, poor Drusilla's won't be around long enough to sag any more than they'd already done."

She knew she shouldn't have responded to him. Good grief. He was completely insane.

Jacob took over again. "I'm a man who likes breasts too, but that's not why we're here, is it, Linus?"

Linus looked at Maggie. "See? He's doing what an interrogator is supposed to do. Find some common ground and get the suspect to think of you as someone just like them."

Ignoring his attempt to draw her into defending her skills, Maggie stared at him with her arms crossed.

"So, back to your dealings with Drusilla. Did you hire her as your accountant?" Jacob asked.

"Yes. Initially, I had her do my taxes, but eventually, she and I decided on a business partnership."

"What did that entail? What kind of business was it?" Jacob asked.

"Before I tell you, are you going to honor your partner's agreement to allow me some extra perks in my cell?"

"Depends on what they are. I can sure agree to more exercise time or more cigarettes and maybe even your own television, but I can't agree to allowing women in your cell if that's what you had in mind."

Linus grinned at Maggie. "See how he did that? Acknowledging that I like women like he does and being gentle as he lets me down in my expectation of females coming to entertain me. That's good for you to learn." After telling Maggie to pay attention to Jacob's actions,

Linus turned to Jacob. "You and I both know—without me confessing to anything at all, mind you—that the kind of female entertainment I would want wouldn't go down well in the prison system."

"So spill it on what you and Drusilla did for a business." Jacob tapped the table with his index finger. "I'm beginning to think you just want someone to keep you company."

"Now, now, Detective, you're getting testy with me like your partner."

"You have to admit, you've been trying to delay giving us what we came for. I have to tell you, we have another person in lockup that we need to speak to. Since you're going to be here awhile, maybe we should go chat with that person first."

"Suit yourself." Linus shrugged. "Is it a man or a woman?"

"Does it matter?"

"Sure. Depending on who it is, I probably have more to offer."

"That's probably true, Linus, but my partner and I need to decide where best to spend our time, and even though I'm enjoying your banter, it seems that all we're accomplishing here is to give you an audience." Jacob closed his notepad and stood.

"It was gemstones," Linus said, as if he were afraid Jacob was headed out of the room.

Jacob sat and opened his pad. "Gems?"

"Yeah. I have a source where I can get them at a good cost. She had some wealthy friends, and we were going to try our hands at selling gems to them. She'd even looked into renting a store and hiring a stone setter to work in the back so we could sell some as already made jewelry for people in a hurry for birthday or anniversary gifts. But most of it was going to be unset stones. Cheaper for us and less chance of customer complaints."

"In what way?" Jacob asked.

"If they bought loose stones and had to take them elsewhere to have them set, we wouldn't be on the hook if a clasp broke or something like that."

"What happened? I presume you, and she never opened that store?"

'Na. Bitch betrayed me. I brought her the gems and, at first, she was selling them on the side and giving me my part as well as the cost of the product. Before too long, she started saying she hadn't had a sale in a while and maybe we needed more variety."

"Did you find out she was stealing from you?"

"She sure was. Never did stop selling. She hid the money and the gems. Did you find them?"

Maggie didn't want Jacob to tell Linus they had the gems but he did. "Yeah, we found them. We also found some gold."

"That's my property. Where'd you find it? I tried to look for it."

"When you murdered her," Maggie asked.

Linus shot her a look then turned back to Jacob. He jerked his hands off the table, rattling his chains. "Is that chick for real? What'd she think I was going to say? That'd I suddenly confess all since you people have my property?"

"I don't think she meant that. I think she wanted to know when you would've been in a position to search for the gems."

"I went to her office to ask her about them. I also visited her house once or twice for the same reason. She denied she was stealing from me."

"And when did you make a search?" Jacob asked.

"Her house when she was at work and vice-versa." Linus grinned. "And there you go, my confession." He snickered. "To breaking and entering."

"You would've never found them in either place," Jacob said. "They were in a bank."

Maggie still couldn't believe her partner was telling the man all of this. Why would he do that? If she were taking lead, she would've said they were right there in her office, and he must've been blind to miss them. That could bait him into admitting he killed Drusilla. If he got mad enough about not finding the gems, he could say more than he intended.

"A bank? What?" Linus wiped his brow. "I didn't think she'd let them out of her sight. She liked to sort them and touch them all the time. I never thought she'd hide them somewhere she couldn't get to them easily."

He was almost ruminating to himself. It was as if he forgot they were sitting there with him.

Jacob leaned over and peered into the suspect's face. "Linus?"

As if startled, Linus jumped a bit in his chair. "Sorry. I was just thinking I didn't realize the woman was that smart. I think I may have underestimated her in her ability to fool me by hiding my property off site."

Maggie didn't think that was particularly brilliant of Drusilla. After all, if she herself had been doing business with some nut job like Linus Anthony, and planned to steal from him, she'd definitely hide the items somewhere where he couldn't have easy access to them if he came looking.

"Not all women are as incompetent as you seem to think," Maggie said.

Linus smirked at her again. "Trust me, doll, they are."

Her blood pressure roared in her ears. She scooted her chair back. It squealed on the concrete floor.

"Going somewhere, babe?" Linus asked.

Ignoring him, Maggie walked out and around the corner to the observation room where Captain Bone stood watching. "Took all you could of that twerp?"

"Good grief, Captain. He's ridiculous. I wanted to leap on him and teach him a lesson."

"He would've enjoyed that. He may have even grabbed one of your puny breasts."

"Very funny." Maggie couldn't help it. She laughed at the captain's words. She helped her calm down and focus on what was happening now that she'd left Jacob alone with the jerk.

"Let's get serious here, Linus, now that Detective Blaine is gone, and you don't have her in here to try to bait."

"Was that what I was doing?"

"Sure it was. We both know it."

"How can you stand having a female partner? I think I'd have to quit the force if they stuck me with one."

"Oh, believe me, I thought about it."

Captain Bone touched Maggie's arm when she started forward at Jacob's words. "Leave it be. Remember, he's saying what the man clearly wants to hear. Linus is definitely a misogynist, and the only way Jacob is going to get him to cooperate is to be the same."

"Yeah, I know that mentally, but it kind of hurts to hear him say it."

"Should you take yourself elsewhere then?"

"No, I need to hear this. I'll be fine." Maggie knew Jacob was doing what was required to get close to Linus, but she really didn't like to hear her partner saying the words. But no way was she leaving. Her desire to see Linus Anthony go down from all they'd seen in his house and the death of Jacob's wife was stronger than her pain at his words.

Her thoughts brought her up short. How much more harmful to his own heart were his words. Linus was the man who took his wife from him, and now Jacob was having to cozy up to him?

Aghast, Maggie turned to her boss. "We need to get him out of there before Linus brings up Debra. That'll be awful and could affect Jacob for the rest of his life."

"I think he's determined to bring Debra's killer to justice. He seems single-minded in that."

"Do you really think any other police department would allow this?" Maggie tried to push down the panic rising in her chest. Her dear partner could be in danger.

"One of the reasons I'm watching and listening to this so intently is to stop it if it looks like it's slipping that way. As you know, I didn't want to even let him stay on the case. He begged me, and I consented, but be sure I've kept a very close eye on him," Captain Bone said.

"Thanks. That makes me feel much better."

The captain pointed at the interrogation room. "Watch."

"Do I need to get an assistant from the prosecutor's office?" Jacob asked.

"Yeah. If you're going to get me the deal, you'll have to. I'll want it in writing and signed off on by both my lawyer and the district attorney." Linus smiled. "You're going to be so glad you offered me this deal."

"What deal?" Maggie asked the captain. "What did we miss?"

Jacob stood. "I'll be right back. I'll need to make some calls."

In a moment, Jacob came into the room. Maggie studied his face. Before he could say a word, she asked, "Are you all right? Being alone in there with Debra's murderer? I shouldn't have left you."

He pulled her into a brief hug. "No, you did the right thing. If you'd have stayed, he'd have continued to harass and show off for you. We'd have never gotten where we are."

"And where are we?" Captain Bone asked. "I'm afraid Maggie and I were talking when you struck whatever deal you struck. I'm sure it's a great one for us, but I'd like to hear it anyway."

"In exchange for not putting a needle in his arm for all the crimes we already have him on, he'll tell us what he knows about Drusilla's death." Jacob wiped his brow.

Maggie noticed his hand shook as he did so. "Are you sure you're all right with this? He should get the death penalty not only for all the women he clearly killed but for Debra as well. Can you stand it that he'll still be living for many years and you helped let that happen?"

"Yes, I can, Mags. I can't be selfish and think only of my wife. I have to think about all those other women. I was able to get him to agree to tell us where he buried them all. So a lot of families will have—not closure because there is never closure as long as your loved one is gone—but knowledge of where the remains are of their wife, daughter, mother, or lover. And the right to bury her." He shook his head. "I *can't* be selfish. As much as I'd like to be there when they insert the needle, I have to make this bargain. For the benefit of everyone."

Wanting to cry at his bravery, Maggie wiped the tears at the corner of her eyes and smiled what she knew had to be more like a grimace. "Well done, partner. Let's hope he actually knows something and follows through on telling where the women are."

"If he doesn't, I'll be first in line to volunteer to drive him to death row."

CHAPTER 13

After the prosecutor and Linus's lawyer met and made the agreement to take the death penalty off the table, Maggie and Jacob were given permission to return to the interview room. The defense lawyer as well as the prosecutor were staying to hear what the suspect had to say.

Maggie spoke to Jacob, "I'll stay in the viewing room with the captain since I don't want to play games with Linus again. Not that I'm afraid or intimidated by him." She smiled. "I think you'll make better progress if I'm not around. He seemed to like trying to impress me. Not that he was impressive at all."

Jacob nodded. "I'll take this on myself. You stay here and watch."

He reentered the room and took his place across from Linus and his attorney who was seated next to his client. The prosecutor stood nearby but didn't engage in the conversation.

"All right. The deal has been made, and now you need to tell what you know about Drusilla Isaacs's death. No more games." Jacob pressed play on the tape recorder on the table. "This is the interview of Linus Anthony. It's three p.m. on Friday, June 24, 2018." He gritted his teeth and continued, "We're on the record now, and once we've got this down verbally, it'll be typed for your signature. Are you ready to proceed?"

Linus leaned in and leered. "I was waiting for the pretty girl to come back. You know, your partner. Is she too afraid to come sit across from me?"

"No, and she's not a pretty girl. She's a law enforcement officer and entitled to the respect of her office, so I suggest you shut your mouth about her."

"You better hope she's not behind that two-way mirror, Detective. She'll be upset with you for saying she's not pretty."

Jacob poked the scratched surface of the wooden table with his index finger. "Nonsense. Are you going to cooperate, or do we put the death penalty back on this table?"

"Just trying to help out a brother. The woman clearly has the hots for you, and you seem unaware of it." Linus sat back in his chair with a self-satisfied smile.

"Never mind. Let's run through what you know about the death." Jacob glared at the suspect. "Last chance."

"All right. You ready?" Linus looked up at the prosecutor who waved a hand at him as if to indicate he needed to get on with it.

"We've been waiting on you, Mr. Anthony, and I can tell you, like Detective Brown said, your time is running out. I'm going to withdraw the offer—" The prosecutor looked at his watch. "—in five minutes, if you don't start talking."

Linus glanced at his attorney and raised his eyebrows.

"Tick-tock, Mr. Anthony." The prosecutor tapped the face of his timepiece. "Tick-tock."

Linus let out a deep sigh. "Fine. You people are all business, aren't you?"

"Look, you may have the rest of your life with nothing better to do than sit in a room, but we all have lives and places to go." Jacob tapped the table again. "Start talking."

"You already know I hired Drusilla to do my taxes and help me with my business records. I told you that. What I didn't say is she was stealing massive amounts of my assets. We had a deal on what she'd be paid but she kept trying to change it."

"And what happened when she tried to change it this last time?"

"I decided I had enough and went over to confront her after leaving her a message that I was on my way." When Jacob opened his mouth to respond, Linus said, "Don't worry, Detective, you didn't miss a clue. You didn't get to hear it because I erased it."

Jacob nodded for him to go on.

"When I arrived, though, her husband was already there. I saw him and that secretary of hers in the side yard, kissing each other."

Making a note of that, Jacob said, "Then what did you do?"

"I went inside and spoke to her about the gems she'd stolen from me. She tried to tell me some stupid story about holding those items safely and that she'd get them to me the next day. I could tell she was lying. Her face was red, and she wouldn't look me in the eye."

"And she was alive when you left?"

A sly grin slid onto his face. "Well, I didn't actually leave then, did I?"

"You tell me. This is your confession, after all."

"Kind of."

Jacob spun his pen on the tabletop. "What's that supposed to mean?"

"I never said I was the one who delivered the killing blow, but I'm trying to tell you what actually happened."

"Then please do," Jacob said.

"Patience, Detective." Linus put his hand up. "I hid behind a set of filing cabinets—you know, the ones that are in front of the entrance to the kitchen area? There's enough room there and in that back corner for a man to stand unnoticed."

"Why did you do that?"

"I figured something was up. What with her being red in the face and her husband and secretary all up in each other's space out there in the yard."

"And was there?" Jacob asked.

"Yep. Sure was. I saw that chick come inside and into the kitchen. She pulled a can of energy drink from the refrigerator, and I saw her dump in some kind of white powder."

"You had a clear view of this, and she never saw you?"

"Don't sound so incredulous, Officer. That little lady was on a quest to harm her boss—and I don't just mean by banging the husband—I mean physical pain or death."

"Okay, for argument's sake, let's say I believe you, what happened then?"

"I'm telling you like it happened. I want my deal, so I'm trying my best to be honest." Linus ran his index finger over his chin, making a rasping noise on his five o'clock shadow.

"So what happened after that?"

"The secretary, Anne, left the room." The suspect glanced around the room. "I stayed where I was for a few minutes, trying to gauge when I could make my move to leave. I had a feeling Drusilla would go to wherever she'd hidden my property. I'd follow and then be able to grab her or my jewels."

"What happened to prevent you from leaving?" Jacob asked.

"That Anne chick called outside for the husband, Curtis. He came in, and she was raving about Drusilla having the guts of a rhino because she wasn't dying."

Jacob looked askance at Linus. "Really? You expect us to believe Anne Leighton was yelling about her boss not dying with her boss sitting right there? Do you think we're idiots?"

Linus splayed his fingers on the tabletop as best he could with them still chained together. "It's what happened. I thought it was crazy too, but then I realized they didn't care what she heard because they weren't planning to allow her to survive."

"You know this because…"

"Because it's what I do, man, it's what I do," Linus said.

His grin was creepy, and Jacob wanted to slug him in the mouth but knew he'd better get control of himself before the captain came in and made him leave. It was already highly unorthodox that he'd been allowed to interrogate the murderer of his wife anyway. He had to toe the line.

"All right. It's what you do. Okay, so tell us what happened after that," Jacob said.

Linus leaned forward. "In a few minutes, I heard

some loud talking, I could tell it was Drusilla's voice, but I couldn't tell what she said. Thinking this could be my chance to get out of the building and hide outside to follow her, I took a step from my spot and then heard the gunshot."

"What did you do then?"

"Stood still while they both ran out of the building."

So now they had the explanation of the poison and the gunshot—if Linus could be believed, that was.

"Once they were gone, I figured I'd go in and have another chat with her."

"What if she was dead?"

"She wasn't. I could hear her crying and wailing. Her words were slurred as I came into her office, but I could still understand her. She pointed to the door and asked me if I'd seen her husband shoot her."

"Did you even think for one moment to call for help?" Jacob asked.

"Hell no, man. Why would I? She wasn't a friend of mine. I didn't care if she lived or died."

"But living, she would've been able to lead you to your gems."

"I know, but you know what?"

"What?" Jacob asked.

Linus leaned back and laughed—a chilling sound. "Sometimes your enemy being dead is better than keeping them alive for the sole purpose of getting your property."

"So what did you do then?"

"When I went in her office, she was standing beside her desk with on hand on the top. She leaned her hip against the side to help her stand. Clutching her gut, she said, 'I need an ambulance,' but I ignored her. I pulled the knife I always carry and stabbed the hell out of that bitch. Over and over." Linus actually made motions as if he were stabbing her again. Or sort of. It was a bit awkward with both hands together.

"And the sign?"

"Sign?" Linus said in an amused way.

"You know what sign," Jacob said.

Linus laughed. "Indeed I do. It fit. She *was* a backstabber. It every way." He stretched his neck toward Jacob and whispered, "I'll have you know, I had a hell of a time getting that note to stick to the blood on her back."

Jacob didn't want to explore that but he knew he needed to. "Let me ask you this then."

"Anything. I'm nothing if not cooperative." Linus nodded.

"How did it end up that Drusilla was stabbed in the back in the first place? You said she clutched her gut and you stabbed her. That sounds like you were facing her so why were the stab marks from the other side?"

"Ahh, see, I'm a real gentleman, Detective. I came to her side and placing my arm around her waist, helped her walk toward the door to her office. She was very unsteady on her feet from the dope and the blood loss, and it made me seem even more helpful."

The expression on Linus's face made Jacob want to strangle him. The suspect was definitely taking pleasure in reliving his crime. It made Jacob sick.

"And just when she thought I was really going to help her, I took the first slice. She squealed like a little newborn oinker." Linus laughed again. "Eventually, she stopped making noise, and I left her there, hoping she'd rot."

"What happened after that?"

"I left but saw the husband lurking in the bushes. I got lucky like I usually do. He didn't seem to see me as he was on his knees looking down at the moment. I thought maybe he was waiting around to see if his wife was going to die, but I soon realized he was sifting through the dirt for something."

"Did you see what it was?"

"I didn't stick around. I wanted to find my own spot to wait to see how long it would take her to die or for someone to come to her aid."

"Where did you go?" Jacob asked.

"There's an apartment complex near there. I went and sat on a patio."

"Just a random patio?"

"No. Of course not. There was a vacant one and someone had left a set of old folding chairs. It was easy to open them and act as if I belonged."

Jacob shook his head. The guy was certainly ballsy. "Did you see anything of interest?"

"I'll say." Linus rattled the chains again. "Drusilla actually made it out of her office. She staggered down the steps, going right past that husband of hers and, obviously not seeing him, kept going down the sidewalk. Then, almost out of nowhere, this chick with a massive amount of muscles—you know, like a bodybuilder—anyway, she comes up and starts screaming something about a little man and Drusilla stealing him from her and then—dang this woman was nuts—the big chick lunges forward, snatches Drusilla by the neck, and bam, twisted it to one side and boom, Drusilla hits the ground, dead at last. I could tell even from where I was." Linus wiped his brow and let out a whistle. "I wanted to run right over and get this muscle chick to teach me how to do that. It was such a great move and, man, it would save me a lot of grief when I'm killing—"

Jacob leapt from his chair so fast, it hit the floor with a clang. As he left the room—before he killed Linus himself—he heard the prosecutor say, "This is Michael Summers, and I'll be taking over for Detective Brown from here."

Glad to be out of the presence of such evil, Jacob slammed the door behind him and took off down the corridor, seeking fresh air and sunshine after the blackness of the interrogation room.

CHAPTER 14

Maggie followed Jacob out of the building. He crossed the road and paced the grassy area near the curb.

After two cars went by, Maggie was able to make her own way to that side of the street. "Are you going to be all right? That guy is some kind of nut job, for sure."

"I'll be fine. I needed to clear my nose of the stench of evil." Jacob ran his hands through his hair. It stuck up everywhere from his actions.

She resisted the urge to reach out and plaster it down.

He continued to breathe hard and didn't seem as if he was going to settle down.

"I'm seriously worried about you." Maggie took hold of his forearm. "You need to relax and try to regroup. I know that's easy for me to say. I can't even imagine your pain in having to go through that with Deb's murderer. Just know I'm here if you want to talk."

"That's the thing, Mags, I didn't *have* to do it. I could've sent you in or Joy Winslow and Jeffery Stutsman." Jacob made a face. "In retrospect, that would probably have been the best way to handle it. I had no business in there with that jerk. Captain Bone should have stopped me."

"Hang on a minute. You insisted on doing that. The captain said she tried to warn you and you ignored her, so don't be saying she should've stopped you. She gave you the freedom to do it, and if she hadn't, you'd be out here complaining she wouldn't let you. Truly, she wasn't in a good situation, no matter how it went down."

"You're right. How do you know me so well?" He gave her a crooked grin. "I'm embarrassed I let that guy get to me. I should've been tougher."

"No. Don't think that way. You're still emotional about what we found in that room in Linus's house. In fact, I think you really handled him well. Better than I was doing." She shrugged. "He wasn't even focused on telling us anything while I was in the room. All I was do-ing was giving him a target for his sliminess."

"It's because you're gorgeous. He can't deal with that. A woman who looks good and has a brain? That's exactly his target victim. I think he was challenged by it and wanted to impress you with his intelligence."

Maggie was stunned that her partner thought she was gorgeous. He'd never said anything of the kind before. They'd been partners and friends for a number of years, but this was different. He'd always treated her as one of the guys, and she had done the same to him. Until that moment she'd woken with him snuggled against her in her bed. She'd had strange thoughts about him since then that she tried to tamp down. She couldn't mess up what they had with some kind of romantic entanglement. And he was still recovering from the renewed angst of his wife's death.

Jacob snapped his fingers in front of her eyes. "Hello? Anyone home?"

"Sorry. I was just thinking."

"About?"

"Getting in the car and going after Curtis Beane's baby-mamma. She of the lycra-wearing, muscle building, neck-breaking fame."

"Linda Matthews?" Jacob asked with a raised eyebrow.

"The very one." Maggie nodded. "As you know, after Winslow and Stutsman questioned her and didn't get anywhere, we had to let her go. Now I'm thinking they were too easy on her.

"Let's do it. Forget about Linus Anthony."

"We're going to have a full jail if we can hang the murder on all four of them."

"I sure hope they all get convicted. Doc said any one

of the methods would've eventually killed Drusilla but I'm sure some of those people will use as their defense the fact that Linda Matthews delivered the kill shot, so to speak."

"I'm sure. Desperate defendants use whatever it takes to try to get off." Maggie pulled her radio from the holster on her belt. She thumbed the receiver to call dispatch. "Can we get a couple of cars to meet us at an address? We're going to need backup as we try to make an arrest."

"Roger." the dispatcher said. "Address?"

"Two-Twenty-Six East Valley Drive." Maggie replaced the radio in its case.

"Do you want to wait for a warrant?" Jacob asked.

Maggie shook her head. "I don't think we need to search her place at this point. We have enough to bring her in for questioning. Linus saying he saw her is enough to ask her a few things."

"Should we call Stutsman and Winslow to go haul in Curtis and Anne Leighton?"

"Yeah, before word gets out. Better to surprise them." Maggie laughed. "Maybe they'll be in bed together. Wouldn't that be fun?'

Jacob shook his head. "You're one sick puppy."

"And you love me for it." Maggie laughed but the laugh was cut short by the look on his face. It was too serious.

"Maybe so. Maybe so," he said as he looked both

ways to cross over to the parking lot. "Come on. Let's go collect our bodybuilder." Over his shoulder as Maggie followed him, he added, "If she doesn't beat us both up and leave us for dead as well."

"No worries, partner. I have a gun, and I'm not afraid to use it."

In the car, Jacob turned the radio on in order to monitor the backup cars. "Let's lag back a little until they're closer to her place. No need in her possibly seeing us and her making a run for it."

"Very true. It'll be easier to take her in the yard so we need to lure her out of the house. She may very well take hostages inside the home if she knows we're coming to get her."

"Good point." Jacob drove on.

Before they arrived at their destination, Maggie's cell phone rang. "Hello?"

"Where did the two of you go?" Captain Bone asked.

"Off to pick up one of the suspects, Linda Matthews. I thought Stutsman was going to tell you. We're sending him and Winslow to grab the others."

"Good plan. Check in when you have our neck-breaker in custody."

"Will do, Captain. Hopefully, it'll be quick and pain-less for me and Brown."

"And not so much for her, right?" the captain asked.

"You didn't hear it from me." Maggie giggled.

They met the officers in the cruiser around the block

from Matthews' house. Maggie got out and leaned in the passenger window of the marked car. "We're going to try to get the suspect outside. We need each of you covering the side and the back."

"Why isn't SWAT coming?" the older officer asked.

"I think I can get her to come out and chat with me. I've already established a relationship with her. If the SWAT truck pulled in and she saw it, that would be the end of it. Get your vests, and if it looks like she won't come, I'll call for SWAT."

"I don't like it, but you're the detective in charge. Your collar, your call."

"Fine. Come along and park a block away so the car can't be seen. It's the second house on the left and is white with yellow shutters."

"Meet you there," the officer said with a shake of his head.

She walked back to Jacob. Getting inside the car, she said, "We have an officer who knows more than me. Better pray he doesn't get shot or break a fingernail. He wanted SWAT out here."

"You have to admit, Mags, taking someone into custody *can* be tricky."

"Don't be wimping out on me, too." She smiled. "I want to kick some rear. I'm tired of being pushed around on this case."

"You haven't been, have you?"

"Maybe not literally but that jerk Linus being such an ass to me has made me hungry for a fight."

Jacob laughed. "Just don't leave any marks on whoever you tussle with."

"I'll try to restrain myself."

Jacob pulled into Linda's driveway. "I'll be right behind you."

"She'll see the car and come out, I hope." Maggie opened the door and put one leg out. "The woman strikes me as the kind who doesn't wait to see who has come to call."

"Come to call? What are you, some kind of duchess?"

"Yep, the Duchess of Glock. Perhaps you've heard of me." Maggie laughed and got out. As she headed up the driveway, she heard him laughing.

Maggie was right in her estimation as the lady of the house stepped out onto her front stoop. Needing her to come out a bit farther to make this easy, Maggie waved. "Good evening, Ms. Matthews. I have some news on the case. Do you have a minute to talk about Curtis?"

"You don't think it was him, do you?" Linda put her hand up to her throat as if shocked. She was still a bad actress, though, and the words didn't sound shocked but more like a bland statement.

"Actually, yes, he had something to do with it."

At this news, Linda fell to the ground and clutched her stomach. "Not my baby's daddy. No, no."

Maggie shook her head. Boy, she was laying it on thick here.

"Are you all right?" Maggie stepped forward and placed one foot on the bottom step.

"I don't know. What will I tell Little Man?"

This was too much. The little man thing again. Lord, was the kid forever doomed to be known as such?

Then Maggie remembered and shook her head in sorrow. The poor kid had no chance with two parents who were immoral and criminals. She hoped for the boy's sake that he had a decent grandparent or two.

"You'll think of something," Jacob said as he came to stand beside Maggie.

Out of the corner of her eye, Maggie could see the officer who spoke to her in the car. He looked as if he were going to make some kind of move. She took a chance and shook her head in his general direction, hoping he would understand it was too soon. They needed to get Linda off the stoop and into the yard. The suspect was still too close to the door and could escape.

Unfortunately, Linda was sharper than she appeared. She leapt to her feet and grabbed the doorknob.

Before she could turn it, Jacob was on the stoop and had his hands on her waist. "Stop."

Linda turned and with a knife that seemed to come from nowhere, stabbed him in the arm. Twisting away, she kicked at him.

Maggie bent forward and grabbed Linda's leg, jerking her to the concrete where she landed on her rear with a hard thud.

The uniformed officers came from each corner of the house, and the younger one pulled Linda's arms behind her back, cuffed her, and began reading her the Miranda warnings.

Looking over at Jacob, Maggie was surprised to see the knife still stuck in his arm. His face white, he said, "I think it's deep, Mags."

She turned to the older officer. "Take Ms. Matthews to the station, and I'll take my partner to the ER."

"Yes, ma'am." He bowed in an exaggerated manner, making Maggie want to punch him in the gut. She just knew he was thinking if SWAT was here, Jacob wouldn't be hurt but hell, if SWAT were here, they'd probably still be staging and dicking around instead of having the woman in custody.

"Mags. I need…" Jacob sat on the stoop.

Worried, Maggie sat beside him. "Can you make it to the car? Do I need to call for an ambulance?"

"I can make it. Don't take out the knife, though. I think it's not going to be good when it comes out."

Maggie helped him to his feet, no longer concerned about Linda Matthews nor Linus Anthony. She had to get help for her partner. It was vital.

The walk to the car with Jacob leaning on her seemed to take forever. She thought it surely must be the way a man walking down the long corridor at death row would feel. Moving at a snail's pace and dreading the end of the journey.

Finally getting him to their vehicle at least five minutes after the squad car left, Maggie opened the passenger side door. "Can you sit up or would you be better off in the backseat?"

"Front is fine." His voice was a mere whisper.

Worried about exactly how deep the knife was and what kind of damage it caused, Maggie put the portable light on the dash and turned on the siren. She was going to get Jacob to the hospital in no time flat if it killed her in the process.

As she drove, she kept shooting glances in his direction. He sat too still for her comfort. His eyes closed, he didn't make any noise except for a moan once in a while as she drove over rough patches in the road.

They finally made it to the ER entrance. Maggie took it on two wheels and pulled into the sally port. Opening her door, she leapt out and yelled for an orderly. "Police officer."

Two EMTs ran out with a stretcher. They eased Jacob out of the car and onto the gurney. He held his hand up and said, "Wait."

"Sir, we need to get you inside," one of them said.

"Maggie?" Jacob turned his head from side to side.

She ran over and stood beside him. "What? You need to let the doctor work on you."

"I need to say something first."

"What? What can be so important? You need to get that knife out. Like now."

"Before I go, I have to tell you…"

"Tell me what? *What?*" Maggie was almost hysterical. Would the man not let them take him inside and see what damage the knife caused?

"I love you. I love you."

The EMT said, "I have to get him inside." Without waiting for an answer, he nodded to the other man and they ran into the building with the gurney between them.

Maggie collapsed onto the curb, with the car still running, door open. He loved her? As in, *loved* her?

CHAPTER 15

It was an hour before anyone came out to tell Maggie what was going on with Jacob. She'd called the captain and was told all the arrests had been made. The case was solved but now what?

What did Jacob mean by saying he loved her? As a partner or in another way? And if it was romantically, what would happen to their partnership?

While it was true that she'd been having odd feelings for him since they'd shared her bed, was that because she was lonely or because she really was in love with him?

Maggie's head was reeling with concern for him and worrying about what he meant.

"The family of Jacob Brown?" A man in scrubs asked.

She stood. "His family isn't here but I'm his partner." Maggie showed him her badge.

"You brought him in?"

"Yes. How is he?"

"He's going to be sore for a while, but he'll recover well enough with some physical therapy. The knife went in deep and cut a tendon, but he'll soon be able to return to the force."

Relief flooded over Maggie. "Thank goodness. Thank you. When can I see him?"

"He'll be in recovery for a while. You may want to go grab yourself some dinner."

"How will I know what room he's in?"

"Just come back up, and the nurse will tell you. Good luck to your partner." The doctor turned and walked away.

Maggie headed toward the elevator. He was right. She was hungry and should call the station again to report on Jacob's condition.

The elevator doors opened, and Captain Bone stepped off. "How's the patient? Any news?" she asked.

"He's going to be okay. Still in recovery. I was going to go to the Subway in the basement and grab a sandwich. You want something?"

"I'll come with you. Give you an update on things."

They went to the cafeteria/food court and found a table once they had their food.

"Did Stutsman and Winslow have any problems with arresting Curtis Beane and Anne Leighton?"

"Nope. They caught them outside the baseball field getting into his car. The only bad part was they had the kid with them."

"How'd our guys learn they were there?"

The captain laughed. "Facebook, of all things."

"Who saw it? I mean who was friends with them that they would see the post?"

"Crazy fools. In this day and age, posting on Facebook with no security protocol. She had zero privacy settings on her wall. Anyone, anywhere, could see what she had there. Posting that you're with your dead boss's husband with his kid at a baseball game is kind of ballsy." Captain Bone stopped and laughed. "I did *not* mean to make that pun."

"What? Ballsy and baseball? I thought it was awesome." Maggie's relief that Jacob was going to be all right made her almost hysterical, and the least thing would have set her off in giggles.

"It *was* pretty good, wasn't it?"

"For sure." Maggie took a sip of her soda. "What's going to happen now?"

"All of them will be charged, and it'll be up to juries to determine who should go down for the actual murder. It's definitely a corker, isn't it?"

"It must be some kind of terrible to be so hated that four people wanted to kill you all on the same day."

"You're right there," the captain said with a laugh.

"God only knows how many more were lined up for the next day, right?" Maggie shook her head. "It's really sad as I used to be friends with her. Drusilla could be nice when she wanted to, but when she turned on you, she was vicious."

"If you don't mind my asking, what happened between the two of you?" the captain leaned forward, obviously eager to hear the tale.

"We had a situation where I was investigating one of her clients and, instead of trying to work with me and see if we could come to some kind of terms, she began this campaign to see me go down. She sent me nasty emails threatening me—"

"Threatening you how?" The captain folded her napkin and placed it beside her empty chip bag.

"To have her client make a report to internal affairs accusing me of misconduct."

"Do you still have those emails?"

Maggie shrugged. "Yeah, probably, but does it matter?"

"No. I was just curious. I'd kind of like to see them so I could maybe understand a bit more about her personality and why she seemed to attract so many enemies."

"I'll let you see them if you promise not to refer me to internal affairs."

"Never. You're a good officer. I'd never believe otherwise."

Tears came to Maggie's eyes at the compliment but also at the memory of why they were here in the first place. "I appreciate the words but my arrogance is why we're here, and Jacob is in a recovery room from surgery. If I'd have listened to the back-up officer and called for SWAT, Linda Matthews wouldn't have had the chance to stab my partner. What if it hadn't been his upper arm but his heart? Or his gut? I could very well be the reason he was dead." Maggie brushed her hair out of her eyes. "And how would I live with myself then?"

Captain Bone reached across the table and patted Maggie's hand. "But he's going to be fine. It didn't happen that way."

"But it could have. What kind of partner am I to put him at such risk?"

"I think the better question is what kind of woman are you that you've fallen in love with your partner and what is your captain going to do about it? Isn't that part of what you're thinking about as we sit here?"

"God. Am I that transparent?" Maggie wiped her eyes, surprised at how relieved she was to have it out there and on the table, so to speak.

"Only to me. I've been watching it happen. Slowly."

"And yet you haven't made us each take new partners."

"No, I haven't, and I won't if it doesn't interfere with your work." The captain held up her hand to silence anything Maggie was going to say. "Yes, the policy manual says I have to do it, but there's also a loophole that puts it within my discretion. Right now, I see a good team, and until I don't, I'm leaving it in place."

"Thank you, not only because I like working with Jacob but because he doesn't know how I feel about him. It would be awkward if you had to tell him we can't be partners because I'm in love with him."

"You *do* know he's in love with you, too, right?" Captain Bone shook her head as if she thought Maggie was the dumbest person on the planet.

"You think so?" No way was Maggie going to share what Jacob said while he was on the gurney. At least not until she found out if he knew what he was saying or if he was merely hallucinating from the pain of the wound in his arm.

The captain nodded. "I know so."

"What about the fact that he just learned who killed Debra? That has to have brought back all those terrible memories from when he lost her. Don't you think he needs to grieve all over again now that he knows who killed her? And has to go through the trial on that?"

"First," the captain held up one finger, "I think Linus Anthony's arrest for the murder of all those women, including Debra, will lead to more healing for Jacob. Now he has the knowledge that will help him move on. He had already come to terms with never finding out the truth, so it's an easy step—in my opinion—to take that information and process it quickly to move past it. I think he's ready for a new relationship, and I truly believe he wants that with you."

"It's pretty scary, though. A big step and maybe a mistake to try to change from what we have to the unknown."

"Speaking of the unknown, let's get back upstairs and see if he's out of recovery." Captain Bone stood and gathered their trash.

When they got off the elevator upstairs, Hattie and John stood at the door.

Hattie scooped Maggie into a hug. "We heard about your partner on the news and thought we better get over here and see what we could do."

Maggie introduced the captain to them, then asked, "How's my friend, Mordecai?"

"We left him eating some left over tuna salad." Hattie put her arm through John's. "My friend here is spoiling my cat. Gonna make him fat."

"You won't let me spoil you, so I'm trying to see if I can win over Mordecai. I figure if I can get the cat to love me, you won't be far behind."

Hattie poked him in the side with her elbow. "Go on with yourself."

Their relationship made Maggie smile. From a sad, lonely woman with only a cat for company a few days ago to a lady flirting with a handsome man, Hattie had blossomed.

Maggie liked to think she had something to do with

their new-found happiness. After all, she'd introduced them.

"We found out Detective Brown is in a room right down the hall here. Come on." Hattie led the way as if she owned the hospital, dragging John behind her.

When they arrived at the room, Maggie held back. What would she find on the other side of that door?

∽∾∽∾

After the captain had a few words with Jacob, and she, Hattie, and John left, Maggie was alone in the room with her partner. She sat in the chair beside his bed and looked down at her fingernails, at a loss for what to say now that there was no one else there.

"What's wrong, Mags?"

"Nothing. I'm glad you're okay. The doctor says you'll have to have physical therapy, but you'll be back to normal soon. I'm so relieved. It was stupid of me to try to get Matthews without SWAT. That patrolman is a better officer than I am. I'm so sorry I led you into danger like that."

"You did no such thing. You're one of the best officers I know. I'd follow you anywhere."

"Don't be ridiculous." Maggie shook her head, still too embarrassed by her new-found feelings for him to make eye contact. "My actions caused your injuries almost as if I'd stabbed you myself."

"That's insane." He patted the side of the bed with his uninjured hand. "Come here a minute. I want to say something while you're on the same level as me."

Nervous, Maggie stood and stepped to his bedside, still unsure where this was going and if he remembered what he said when he was in shock and pain from the stab wound.

She leaned her hip on the side of the mattress.

Jacob took her hold of her hand. "The doctor said they would let me out of here early in the morning if I did well tonight and had someone at home to take care of me. He doesn't want to release me if I'll be alone as I'm only going to have the use of one arm for a while."

"If you're asking if you can stay with me, you know you can. You've been spending every night at my place for a long time. Coming home for me to help take care of you is not a problem."

"Are you sure? After all, I don't want to cramp your style if you wanted to go on a date or something. Me coming over at bed time and using your guest room is a little different than me moving in for a while."

"You really think I want to go on dates? With who?" She couldn't process what he was saying. Had he truly forgotten what he said? Or was he trying to give her an out? Letting her pretend she didn't hear it?

He shrugged one shoulder. "I don't know, Mags. We've never really talked about it. I know you get asked out a lot. Hell, I bet that new crime scene guy, James, has flirted with you and asked you to dinner."

"Yeah, he has sometimes seemed to be flirting, but I'm not interested."

"I heard some of the women talking about how hot he is. Why aren't you interested?"

"Listen up, Jacob," Maggie said, frustrated at the way the conversation was going after the captain had planted the idea in her head that she and her partner could be more than merely work partners. "Are you playing games or did you mean what you said when they wheeled you into this building earlier today?"

His smile appeared tentative. "It depends."

"On what?"

"Can I explain something to you?"

"Of course. You know you can." Maggie tried to ease the tension. "Unless it's some algebraic equation. Then that's a big no."

"I'm serious here, Mags."

She nodded. "All right, no more joking. Go ahead."

"We've been partners a long time. Even when Deb was alive. And as you know, I've always had the greatest admiration for you."

Maggie couldn't help but think this sounded like a break-up talk but she refrained from saying so.

"I never thought my marriage would end, and I certainly never thought it would be with the murder of my wife."

Maggie squeezed his hand. "Me either."

"What I'm trying to say is if Deb had lived, I would never have been in the position I am now."

"I know. I know. You wouldn't have dashed out of the Linus Anthony interrogation and been stabbed at my arrest scene."

Jacob frowned. "That is *not* what I'm saying."

"Then what exactly are you trying to communicate here? You've never been one not to be able to form words? Why now?"

"Because once I say what I want to say, it can't be unsaid. Things will never be the same."

"If what you want to say will make things better, then say it. If it won't, then don't." Maggie wasn't sure she wanted to hear his words. She was as torn as he was. She did, but she didn't.

"That's the thing. I don't know."

"Then tell me, and we'll decide together." Maggie's gut clenched as he tightened his grip on her hand so hard she thought he would crush the bones.

"If Deb were still alive, I would never have looked at another woman. I'm a committed man, and she was the woman I married. To me, that meant she was forever." Jacob stared at Maggie for a moment. "But then she was killed, and I found her. I was smothered in guilt and lost for a time. You were amazing as my partner and even let me come to stay with you when I found I couldn't sleep in my own home. I was grateful to you and for a very long time, I thought that was all I felt. Gratitude."

"I was happy to be there for you." Maggie smiled.

"But then, while this case was going on, and after we found all that horror at Linus's house, things changed." He nodded. "That night you comforted me and allowed me to sleep in your bed, I started to look at you in a different way."

Maggie wanted to make a joke about how she must have looked with bed hair since she always used humor to deflect serious conversations but she reined herself in as Jacob was so intense.

"I tried to fight my feelings but it was no use. Every day when I'd first see you, my heart leapt in my chest and I couldn't keep the smile off my face."

"I noticed you actually seemed more positive in the mornings than you had in a long time." Maggie smiled and hoped he would keep talking. She needed him to say those all-important words.

"Mags, I know we've always been friends and colleagues and kept things on a professional level, but I find myself wanting to be anything but professional and anything but a colleague. I find myself wanting to kiss you until we're both senseless. But at the same time, I'm scared to death that you'll reject me and think I'm pathetic."

"There's not one thing about you that's pathetic."

He gave a wry smile. "Even my inability to sleep in my own house?"

"Look, I wouldn't even be able to go inside a house where my loved one was killed, much less sleep there. I can't even imagine dealing with that every day so that is completely *not* pathetic."

"I didn't hear a response to my need to kiss you."

Instead of saying anything, Maggie leaned forward and placed her lips on his.

Jacob let go of her hand and, placing his unwounded arm around her waist, pulled her closer. His tongue slid across her lower lip, causing her to gasp.

When her mouth was open to him, he deepened the kiss and ran his fingers up her spine.

Maggie shuddered and let herself fall into the kiss with all her being. The man had magic in his tongue, that was for sure.

He kept his arm around her. How had she never known he was so muscular? His thinness disguised the strength in him.

"Ahem," a voice startled them, and they broke apart.

Jacob laughed. "Good evening, Nurse. I was taking my medicine."

"Interesting meds you got there, Detective. How about taking the ones I brought? You know, to stave off infection." The nurse had a little paper cup she rattled in front of him.

Jacob winked at Maggie. "You know, I'll be glad to

take those, too but I was having my spoonful of sugar first."

"To help the medicine go down?" the nurse asked.

"Delightfully." Jacob took the proffered meds and swallowed them with some water from his bedside Styrofoam cup.

The nurse made a note in his chart and turned to Maggie. "We need to let the patient get some rest."

"I'll be leaving soon." Maggie wasn't going to let the woman bully her out of the room until she was ready to go. Heck, she knew plenty of people who stayed all night by the bedside of their loved one in the hospital. She'd do so too if she wanted.

"Don't tarry too long," the nurse said on her way out.

As soon as she was gone, Maggie said, "Who does she think she is? I'll stay all night if I want."

"Are you guarding me?" Jacob grinned.

"You bet I am. No pretty little blonde nurse is going to tell me what I *have* to do."

"If I didn't know better, I'd think you were jealous. It's not like she wants to date me, Mags."

"You don't know that. I saw how she was assessing you. Men don't notice these things."

"Remember one thing about me, my love," Jacob said.

"Your love?"

"Isn't that what I just told you?"

Maggie shook her head. "I didn't hear anything about loving me."

"God, woman. To be so smart and a detective to boot—one who solves crimes so well and can tell when a nurse is assessing a patient for dating purposes—you can be dense. I told you I was a one-woman man. And right now, you're that woman."

"Right now?"

He smiled. "And forever. If you'll have me."

"I think I'll take forever."

"Starting now?"

She shook her head. "No, starting tomorrow when I can take you home and have you share my bed for real. And I mean not just for sleeping."

"Lock that door over there, baby, and let's start forever now."

Maggie grinned and sauntered over to the door. The heck with the blonde nurse.

It was time to see exactly how magical Jacob could be, and there'd be no waiting for tomorrow for her. She was never going to be lonely again. He was always true to his word, and if he said she was the woman for him, she knew it was true. And it didn't hurt that she loved him, too.

The End

About the Author

Sherry Fowler Chancellor is a practicing attorney who lives on the beautiful Gulf Coast of Florida. When she's not working on behalf of her clients, she's busy penning a new story or hanging out with her friends and family in their own little slice of paradise.